About the Author

Peter Pietri is an author who lives with his dog Buddy in Raleigh, North Carolina. He is passionate about writing, photography and programming video games. He has been writing stories since childhood and worked on Redemption for five years during college and finished the novel in 2020 during COVID. Peter is an advocate for strong female characters and this fully manifests in the story of Aylene Candent, who bears an enormous burden but is gifted with spiritual powers and tremendous shifts of fate.

Redemption

Peter Pietri

Redemption

Olympia Publishers
London

www.olympiapublishers.com
OLYMPIA PAPERBACK EDITION

A CIP catalogue record for this title is
available from the British Library.

ISBN: 978-1-80074-957-3

This is a work of fiction.
Names, characters, places and incidents originate from the writer's
imagination. Any resemblance to actual persons, living or dead, is
purely coincidental.

First Published in 2023

Olympia Publishers
Tallis House
2 Tallis Street
London
EC4Y 0AB

Printed in Great Britain

Acknowledgements

I would like to thank my mother Anna, my sister Alethea and my best friend Jessica in equal parts. The three of you bring meaning to my life and form my superb support network. Thank you for everything you've done for me. Francisco, thank you for being a first reader. I couldn't do it without you, brother. I lastly want to acknowledge all of the women in the world who feel like they aren't main characters, or aren't represented well in stories. I promise that the story of Aylene Candent and her journey for redemption will be one you never forget.

Chapter 1

The Academy

It was my first day at the Academy. The Glass Castle, walls and towers of a swirling, mystic shimmer. Totally translucent until the touch of your fingertips resolved the smooth, white alabaster inlaid with silver. I was just seventeen at the time. Young to have enrolled in the Academy, but not exceptionally so. I still remember that day as vividly as the coloured crests of silk which adorned the walls around the castle. All I could think about was how big the damn place was. Too many rooms! Too many. More hallways and closets and courtyards and this-ways and that-a-aways and maybe-here's than a girl could ever hope to count. I was younger, then. Still eager, easily excitable, quite pleased at my having been admitted to study in the same stone halls as my family before me.

Standing at the high stage at the back of the chapel was Grand Magister Hardbub. Stout of stature, but even larger of character. It was one of those moments you ought to pay attention to. The candles in the chapel were ornate as everything else, a rainbow of colours and gold and silver bases. The windows were stained glass, intricate and depicting myths and lore from times forgotten. I remember noticing the professors' cloaks, the curious colours and matching hats and odd accessories, the purpose and history of which I've yet to come to know. At the time, I was busy searching the crowd of faces, looking for the few good friends and the talented rival I hoped and needed to make. A deafening applause. Everyone had stood up and was clapping. Except for me, as it happened; I was the last one to join in. I was a little stunned to be there at all.

A few of the girls near me noticed, but thankfully it was too loud for me to hear their laughter. I blushed red and looked away from them, scanning the crowd and stopping only when my eyes accidentally met the gaze of a tallish and yet unassuming fellow. His eyes were light brown, his hair medium-length and dirty-blond. He had a soft handsomeness, an air of dignity which seemed mellowed by kindness. I figured he must have been around three years or so older than me. I decided he was most likely a sophomore and I was surprised and pleased when he smiled towards me and greeted me with a friendly nod. I felt shy but smiled back before turning to face the clapping crowd and our Grand Magister who stood proudly at the head of the aged chapel.

For some three centuries the Academy had been sharpening the minds and honing the abilities of mages such as myself. Prestigious, rigorous, an institution which was known for procuring and training only the most talented of magi. Our grounds were to the West of Boston, at the top of a hill shrouded by a forest on reserved land, the appearance of which was obscured by arcane magic. The laypeople knew nothing of us, and yet we sat and stood beside them on their subways. We took their taxis, we rode their planes, or rather, we did so when we chose to enjoy the slow tranquillity of conventional travel.

The Grand Magister began reciting the First Oath. Hands on our hearts and our faces solemn, we stood in front of him and repeated the words which had guided our people for as long as we've kept records of history. *Our Minds, Our Magic, Our Hearts, Our Honora. Our Light to Break the Darkness!* Oath taken, words spoken, the upperclassmen and professors applauded in recognition of the new members of the Academy. A third of us, perhaps, would graduate. Of those that didn't, some would transfer to the lesser but still rather important institutions which trained lower-ranking members of the Arcane Guard.

I could sing a song of praise for the food, for the fresh fruit, for the roasted chicken and lemon potatoes and the eclectic assortment of delicacies and delights our dining hall offered. Not like laypeople colleges; as far as I'd heard their food was usually terrible. No, we were fortunate to have many comforts and luxuries, at least when it came to food. Without them even fewer of us would make it through our training. But on that day, that Sunday towards the end of August, the day before class would start, it was hard to appreciate my first tasting of the quality of the food.

It was hard because, after filling my tray, I went to sit down at a table occupied by what I thought were friendly faces. They'd been smiling and laughing amongst each other, at least they did until they noticed me approaching. Immediately, the four occupants sat up and took their trays with them, leaving briskly so as to avoid any association. One girl, of pale skin, with green eyes and unnervingly straight hair, decided she'd have a go at me. She put her tray back on the table and stood aggressively, facing me with dagger eyes and obvious repulsion. She spat at me in much the way a member of aristocracy ought not to.

A silverish blue glow emanated from my hand, and with it came the telling ting. I reflected and amplified her spit back towards her. A half moment later and it looked like an elephant had sneezed all over her face. It was a face that after a few

11

moments, I recognized. She was Trisha Tornett, heiress to one of the formerly seven (now six) Great Houses. My heart was pounding. I felt adrenaline surging through my veins. She was mortified, her cheeks were red with embarrassment, and she looked like she wanted to kill me. Her friends looked shocked too, but they just stood there. Students at all of the tables turned around and watched us, knowing who we were. I'm sure we must have been a curious sight for them. A few still-then strangers laughed nervously, as if to break the tension of the total silence as Trisha and I stood in opposition.

Trisha's hands began glowing silver and then her face was cleaned, instantly immaculate as she liked it to be. Her emerald eyes were burning with anger and hate she had likely felt for me for many years. Fiery red then surrounded her hands which spread open in indication that she intended on roasting me, like the chicken that they were serving that day.

"Fight! Fight! Fight!" Students around the dining hall were egging us on.

I was as proficient at casting Barrier as could be expected of a mage my age. Better, even. But Trisha was older, stronger - that was obvious just from the sight of the black sparks which started crackling in her flames. Along with the sight of her flames were distant memories of visiting her family's castle when I was just a little girl. She was three or four years older than me... I remember seeing her use Colorshift with ease when I could barely use Bubblebreath.

A sunburst flash blasted against the clear sheen of my barrier, sizzling for a few seconds before dispersing. I'd stopped it. Barely. Her force was such that I slid back several feet even with my blocking. Two, maybe three, if I was lucky. Two or three brief defensive moments were all that stood between me and her flames melting my face.

I'd live, probably, if only because at least a few other students would likely have the decency to surge me with enough mana to maintain my life force. But I didn't and don't consider myself to be particularly beautiful, and in those moments, I was quite worried as to what the sight of me would be afterwards. In hindsight, I should have called her bluff. She knew I'd block her first shot, her second. She'd lessen her third if only to not risk maiming me, and ending up in a magi prison. No, she'd have just given me a good singeing, obviously. I was worth less than the worms that dug through dirt, to her. Her pride wasn't worth what would become of her.

Even so, at that moment, I wasn't thinking logically. My heart was still pounding and I felt sick. I had goosebumps and I could practically feel the heat of her fireballs on my cheeks. Then came the signature warning glow which always preceded the outward burst of a cast of Fireball. Silence. No one was cheering. Silence.

The silence was broken by a barely perceptible crackle of her flames which only the two of us and her friends were close enough to hear.

"Are you ready to see the light, Candent?"

"Are you?" I said back, snapping at her the way a wiser mage wouldn't.

With bravery, with stupidity, I sprinted towards her as fast as I could. I'd honed my magic over the years, but I was an athlete too. Sound body, sound mind, sound spirit. The slight glow tracing my aura was the sole indicator of my channelling Lightswift, amplifying my speed to such an extent that my dash towards her would have been barely perceptible to the untrained, unmagical eye. Trisha's eyes widened, more with hate than fear, and her lips curled in a sinister smile. She brought her open hands together for a double-cast. If I was to attack her, she would respond to me without mercy. She would call it self-defence and incinerate me, and knowing her status, she'd probably end up getting away with it. Who would testify on *my* behalf?

The light blue flash of death, the unnerving glow of a flame more than hot enough to instantly vaporize flesh. A sound difficult to describe to a layperson, soft as the burst of a bubble, horrifying because it comes simultaneously with that fireball just slower than the speed of sound. The roar of the flame expanded into a chaotic explosion. I warped far enough to the right that her fireball missed me, but it was so hot she burnt my arm, anyways. That's how powerful she was. In that same moment, as I warped out of the way, as I felt the heat of her fire blast burn my arm, I put all of my force into a double-casted Windblast. I sent her back against the wall. There is the crackle of flame, and then there is the whoosh of a wind-tossed adversary.

Feeling and ignoring the medium burn on my arm, I left the dining hall. I walked, unhappy, weakened and sore, to the dormitory where I would live with two other students. Our beds, unfortunately, were not very comfortable, at least not when your arm has second-degree burns. Our rooms were not large, especially for three people. My roommates, as it happened, were not particularly friendly.

Not to me, anyways. It seems my family's history had yet to be forgotten, understandably so. My conflict with Trisha didn't help, either. Everyone was talking about it. I'd walk into a room or through a corridor and students stared at me and whispered. Damn. I was still unpacking my clothes and arranging my miscellaneous belongings when I met the two girls with whom I was assigned to live with for nearly a year.

The black-haired girl looked shocked to see me. Her eyes widened when I turned to face them... but she said nothing. Standing beside her was a blond girl with a pretty face and angelic sky-blue eyes which seemed both innocent, and somehow devious. I could tell that the two of them already knew each other, and the blond one in particular seemed to hold a resentment towards me. I felt a tinge of sorrow at the possibility of a direct connection between my life, and the loss of her loved one.

My clothes were quite juxtaposed with theirs. I was wearing bronze raiment, simple and standard issue for recruits without the money for fancier and prettier things. They were dressed like ladies, velvet and lush raiments, where mine was rugged, and their faces were adorned with make-up. They had the subtle blush and lipstick and their long hair perfectly straightened except for the intricate, traditional braids at the top. I wondered if they had already heard about what happened.

"You shouldn't be here," said Elizabeth, the girl with the blond hair.

Samantha nodded her head in quiet agreement, crossing her arms in clear opposition to my presence.

"My family helped found this school," I said, defiant and defensive.

Elizabeth laughed and then I realized how foolish my words had been, all things considered. Her laughter and my quietness said more than enough, and Samantha stood there in frowning agreement.

"Don't touch our things," said Elizabeth, "You've taken enough from us all already."

I looked away and assured them that I wouldn't, and then I left. It was only the first day. I'd barely been on campus, I'd yet to unpack and organize my belongings, and I was already quite unpopular. The fight, my father's sin... I had come to seek redemption and I already felt as though my efforts would be in vain. As I did on many such days, I left my room, I navigated the corridors through and past the halls and eventually found the courtyard. It was on the top of the castle, and it was up more flights of stairs than most students cared to climb. It was accessed through the Vault which was protected with glyphs that supposedly suppressed all forms of magic.

The Glass Castle had been built around the Vault. The arcane library was filled with laypeople books, common tomes, ancient scrolls and forbidden grimoires of magic, the casting of which could result in a death sentence. More magic texts than a mage could study in three lifetimes. A collection so large that each floor of the library descended to another, down a flight of stairs, down and down again. Floors and floors of written knowledge, hidden passages, warp points to unknown and forgotten places. It was at the very top that I found the courtyard.

Lilac trees with bluish flowers. Bushes and shrubs with leaves which curled like ice cream swirls or curly hair. Roses of every colour and orchids which seemed as if they came from a science-fiction movie. Some of the trees had apples, or at least I think they were apples. Red and green, yellowish, orange like a bell pepper and even fuzzy-looking ones that looked like they thought they were peaches and failed in their attempt to mimic one. I thought about eating one, but I didn't know much about botany or herblore and I wasn't quite sure which, if any, were poisonous. It wouldn't be a stretch, given my luck. I'd been poisoned before.

But I very much enjoyed the courtyard. The familiar floor of marble, the benches on which one could sit and take in the sights and the smells. There was the light breeze which almost always blew. Aeromagic worked to keep the weather on campus mostly pleasant year-round, even in the winter months. I could already tell I would find myself frequently at this courtyard, my flowered sanctuary. Each time I'd sit, watching from above, looking down upon the campus grounds, at the forest and other-student gazing. It was like a watercolour painting I never felt a part of.

As he would, on many such occasions, Tobias Racond approached me as I sat on what would become my usual bench. It had been many years since I had seen him. His hair was long as mine, shoulder-length and dusty brown where mine is more reddish. His hair was wavy and he had those dark eyes, so unalike my red eyes, his looked not at you, but past you, and occasionally glowed with fire. He was wearing silk raiment, crimson and black with shoulder hoods. His silk shirt and pants were not gaudy but tasteful. Even with the golden buttons engraved with the Dragon crest of his house. His eyes met mine, and he had a sly smile, a subtle curl at the top of his mouth, like a smirking fox.

"I watched your fight, Candent," said Tobias.

"What of it?" I asked.

Tobias ran his fingers through his hair and brushed a lock back behind his ear. His black eyes sparkled with red and gold; there was Dragon in his blood. Tobias' ancestors had fused their souls with Dragons. The burn on my arm, which was healing slowly, flared for a brief moment as he spoke.

"She nearly killed you," he said, his voice calm and quiet, but his radiating energy gave him away.

I shrugged. "Well she didn't. I am more than capable of defending myself."

Tobias ignored my words but responded airily "I considered intervening, you know. I wouldn't have minded killing her and saving us both the heartache."

My eyes widened with shock and disgust.

"There's something seriously wrong with you," I said. "And anyways, it happened way too fast for you to have stopped her."

Tobias smiled as I sat there, quiet, not truly frightened… but certainly a little disturbed. I was pretty sure, or at the least was hoping, that he was joking, perhaps poking fun at their betrothal. I looked at his face, narrow, his features striking, his cheekbones sharp and high. He was prettier than me. He looked like he belonged in one of the myths on the stained glass of the chapel. He'd have an ash-grey staff, sinister, whitish hair from Death Magic and lives taken, and violet waves swirling around his hand like a corrupted Alven; a Dark Arcanist.

The Dragon moved his hand towards me slowly, his palm open. The light hairs on the back of my neck raised and I felt goosebumps all over my body. I tried not to gulp nervously but did so anyways. A red rose, no thorns, materialized between his fingertips as he closed his hand and offered it to me. I'm not sure why I did, but I accepted the flower. It wasn't until much later that day that I would contemplate how it was that he casted magic in spite of the magic suppression.

"You have many enemies, Candent," said Tobias. "But I am not yet one of them."

Chapter 2

Friends and Foes

Imagine my surprise when the next morning I walked into the training hall for my first course, Projection II: Offensive Magic, and saw Trisha Tornett. As a particularly talented junior, she had, apparently, been selected by Professor Darvek to serve as a teacher's assistant. I was the first student to walk in and, immediately, from across the room, she turned and saw me. The professor wasn't in yet, and Trisha's green eyes flashed with threatening magical wisps. Her lips curled into that evil smile that I suspected I would often see. We stared each other down in an uncomfortable silence as I walked to one side of the hall.

The room had six sides, an odd hexagon of cobalt blue but slightly-clear bricks, Manastone enchanted so as to endure the arcane abuse from magi in training. Bowling-ball sized Shinequartz crystals, spread out evenly and floating up near the ceiling, filled the room with slightly purple and annoyingly-bright illumination. I very much hoped I would get used to it. I didn't want to be standing around and looking squinty and stupid when the rest of my classmates entered. The silence of animosity between Trisha and I was absolute except for the humming of the Shinequartz above us. Professor Darvek entered the room, followed closely by a few especially eager-looking students, two girls and a boy.

Darvek was a rather small fellow, almost a head shorter than me, with most of his face covered by cartoonishly large, full-moon shaped sunglasses. Rosy cheeks, short black hair spiked up like little blades of alert grass, and he had a black and neatly-trimmed goatee. No robes, he was wearing laypeople clothes; skinny white jeans and a sleek form-fitting grey jacket and matching sneakers which combined the colours. A quick upwards flick of his head acknowledged me, and he saluted Trisha with a casual lifting of his hand. Darvek walked towards the podium and then took his place, speaking, his voice amplified by magic such that it boomed throughout the chamber.

"I'm quite pleased to see the two of you, early as it is," he said. "It says a great deal about a student, to arrive early. It shows dedication."

Darvek stayed at his podium, standing and grinning, waiting for the rest of the class to arrive. More students trickled in, some nervous, some sleepy, a few with that magic spark in their eyes so indicative of strength of will and ambition. I studied their faces as they entered, and it seemed that many if not most of them recognized me. Friend, entirely indifferent to my existence, or perhaps even soon to be foes. I wasn't sure, I couldn't tell. I supposed it likely that they had already heard about my... skirmish... with Trisha.

I wondered if they recognized her already too, and if they did, what they were thinking. And if they didn't, well, perhaps the months to come would serve as a source of entertainment for them. A hellish circus of lightning, manabolts, an inferno of fireballs colliding with and bursting against barriers on a daily basis. Darvek the ringleader, egging us on, teaching us all new spells and encouraging practice and independent studies in the Vault. Maybe he would say to me, *yes, Aylene, she is older than you, and stronger, but who's to say there isn't an incantation for you to stumble upon to give you an edge in battle?* Or maybe not; maybe he would work to maintain the order of the classroom, if only to prevent the haphazard immolation of an innocent and unsuspecting bystander.

Instead of a lengthy introductory speech, Darvek opted for showmanship and pizazz, two arms thrown into the air and a waggling of the fingers. A bright flash of white light overpowered the purple of the room before morphing into a menagerie of shimmering swirls and colours. Total chaos which solidified as distinct figures and patterns. His magic had filled the room with the sensory explosion of a three-dimensional mosaic of awe-inspiring geometric impossibilities. Gasps of wonder, the fizzle of dancing magic.

The faint buzzing of the Shinequartz Orbs floating above us sounded like an old electric appliance in the background. There is the clumsy clay pot of a novice art class, and there is the pottery master's amphora, and so it is with magic. There are simple emanations of crude mana, an ordinary fireball, a blast of wind; and there are those spells of such intricacy that only a few magi in the world have mastered them.

During this first class session, Darvek referenced some of the spells we would be working on over the semester. Additional practice with Manabolt; sweet and simple, that quick zap to stun an unprepared foe. The trusty Fireball; powerful, but instead of launching wasteful explosions of excess, we would focus on control and speed. A volley of ten smaller fireballs is far harder to block or deflect than one big one. Windblast; to stagger an opponent and knock them back with invisible winds, much harder to block than Manabolt. Fastflash; an explosion of magic light to blind an enemy (unless they had on a good pair of sunglasses, as Darvek pointed out with a cheeky grin). Lightsphere; a spell with a base incantation similar to Fastflash but instead you conjured a ball of light to follow you and illuminate the darkness.

Voidburst; Professor Darvek informed us that this would be the most technical of the spells that we would work on. Instead of projecting an elemental energy, like electricity, you formed a point of pressure and expanded the wave radially in all directions. It's a highly efficient technique, it's quite effective at deflecting attacks, and it's one of the most potent standard spells in the magi arsenal.

"If a mage was to conjure a precisely-controlled and high-magnitude Voidburst, at the very centre of an enemy," said Darvek, asking the class, "what do you suppose would happen?"

The professor looked around, his grin replaced by a more solemn look, studying our faces as we pondered. No one answered. We looked around at each other. Trisha was smirking from her position near Darvek with her arms crossed. I raised my hand and answered, suggesting that the little energy it took to cast Voidburst would be negated by the defending mage's aura.

"Interesting," he said, his face and tone saying little. "That is supposing their mana is not drained. There are a handful of other variables to consider as well. Would anyone else care to offer an alternative hypothesis?"

A freckled girl, who was dark-skinned, like me, raised her hand and answered in a timid voice, pushing up her glasses as she spoke. Her guess was similar; she supposed that casting Voidburst at another mage would be impossible because each of us has a different manarate. Our energy pulses through our bodies at different speeds, like a fingerprint, so pure mana would be incompatible with your manafield and could not pierce it. The mana for the Voidburst would be converted into light or deflected away.

"Would anyone care to explain to..." said Darvek as he looked around. "Excuse me, lassie, what's your name?"

"Madison," she said, blushing.

"Would anyone care to explain to Madison, and Aylene," he said, "why the two of them are wrong?"

My cheeks went warm with a blush as the rest of the students looked around.

A few were mumbling but none had the courage to offer an alternative answer. Well, no one except for Tobias, who had apparently been standing among us the entire time. I was *pretty* sure I hadn't seen him walking in, but maybe I had missed him. Or maybe he'd been using Illusion Magic. Tobias answered the professor, not waiting to be called on, his voice controlled and resonating with magic amplification.

"Madison's hypothesis is, unfortunately, entirely incorrect," said Tobias. "Or else Manabolt wouldn't be a spell."

Professor Darvek sighed and rubbed his forehead. If he was happy to see Tobias it certainly didn't show in his face. Madison looked absolutely petrified, and Tobias' frigid tone of nonchalant indifference was such that the students closest to him shuffled further away.

"I wasn't aware that you were enrolled in this course," said Darvek, frowning. "In fact, considering that I am a member of the Projection department's faculty, I am quite sure that you recently received approval to begin working on independent research."

Tobias shrugged. Trisha glared at him and suggested to Darvek that she could escort Tobias, by force, if necessary, out of the training hall. Tobias said with a deadly calmness to Trisha, and to the class, that she would not survive the attempt. Trisha scoffed and looked indignant, turning to Professor Darvek, who responded to her with a coldness that almost matched Tobias.

"I've no interest in your Highborn romance and political drama," said Darvek. "You're more than capable of defending yourself, Trisha, and as for you, Mr. Racond, I'm quite sure your time would be better spent elsewhere, as opposed to threatening your peers."

At the back of my mind, I was still wondering what the answer was to Darvek's question about Voidburst. As a Projection class studying offensive magic, if we were studying the spell, I supposed the answer to be rather unpleasant. I raised my hand to further inquire, and Trisha, who had been glaring at Tobias, turned and snapped and answered my question. Trisha explained that Manabolt grows in potency when the caster has a faster manarate than the defender, and the same goes for Voidburst.

If you're significantly faster, or if your opponent is out of mana… they explode from the inside out. Yikes. We spent the rest of class practicing with Voidburst to deflect small, precise fireballs. In case you are curious, the incantation for most fire spells is in Draconic, and the focal points of the rune (a sort of geometric hodge-podge) correspond to the syllables of the word as with most incantations. If you develop mastery of the spell, like almost any spell, you can say the words not with your mouth, but in your mind. Note that you capitalize the name of spells, but not the particular cast of a spell itself. For example, Fireball is a spell and so its name is sacred, although we do not reveal the divine word itself, but you don't capitalize a particular fireball that is about to hit you.

On the way out of class, I overheard a few students gossiping about Trisha and Tobias. Technically speaking, as much as I doubted it would ever happen, if Tobias and Trisha acted in accordance with Highborn tradition, they had been betrothed since *birth*. They would have to get married one day. The Gilded Dragon and the Serpent. How little I envied their Highborn ways and woes!

One of my other courses was Defensive Magic I. Before the course, I could cast a few barriers, strong ones, but I wasn't proficient enough in Redirection or Absorption to skip the introductory course. The professor, High Mage Redsby, was a blond woman as haunting as a skeleton and nearly as thin. Light blue eyes, hair in a tightly-knotted bun, violet raiment with red trim and silver buttons. A noblemage but not one of the Royal Seven.

That day, about two weeks into my first semester, my sparring partner was Herbert Hardbub, the handsome fellow with the dirty-blond hair whose name revealed him as being the Grand Magister's son. I was quite surprised when I saw him in the first class session, and even more surprised when I realized who he was. They resembled each other, sort of. Harold Hardbub was a little bit shorter, and quite a bit wider. The Hardbub crest is the 'Boar and Truffle'. They are widely-known as a merry and indulgent sort of people, a generalization it seemed our nation's leader took to heart (cholesterol included).

Handsome and always smiling warmly, the more I observed Herbert in class, the more goofy I came to know him to be. He was terrible at magic. Terrible. In all honesty, although I only had this course with him, I couldn't fathom how he'd even been admitted to the Academy. A sweetheart, he'd be at home in a candy shop, as a partaker or the cheerful merchant. But he wouldn't stand a chance against Da'raakan or even the measliest of his Demons and Shadow Mages. Were his father not the Grand Magister, I imagine he'd have had to attend college with the laypeople.

Most of his attempted redirections failed to cast, manifesting only as a disappointing silverish glow and a half-hearted bleep. Occasionally, he was successful... sort of. We were supposed to redirect the manabolts to the target statues, not our peers, who were more than happy to respond in kind with manabolts of their own.

On one hand, I was sort of excited to practice with Herbert and get to know him. But Professor Redsby was very strict, and we couldn't really talk much during class. But if we trained together, I'd at least have something to start a conversation about. On the other hand, he really was awful, and I didn't want to accidentally hurt him or embarrass him. He was so much taller and bigger than me, the sight of me knocking him down must have looked really ridiculous.

Manabolt is one of the first attack incantations mages learn and practice. It's kind of odd; it crackles and stings like electricity, and it sounds like a high-pitched 'bzzp'. It's relatively easy, it's efficient, and we were also instructed to practice it as part of Projection. For most mages at the level we were at, it was pretty much just a quick zap, like someone pushed you in the chest just hard enough for you to lose your balance and stumble backwards. Because manarate directly correlates (with a few genetic exceptions) with a mage's age, students around the same age produce manabolts which are able to pierce each other's aura. Unfortunately, for Herbert, Manabolt isn't really a spell which you can moderate the strength of. Its strength is determined by your manarate: the frequency at which your mana flows through your body. The larger the difference between your and your opponent's manarate, the more powerful the zap. Bzzp.

Herbert, for the eighth time in a row, was unsuccessful in his attempt to redirect my manabolt. Each time my bolt hit him in the chest he slid back a few feet and wobbled, barely able to stop himself from falling over. We were only halfway through the class. And that was with the multiple breaks and the five or so times our professor came over and tried to coach him. He was dripping with sweat, his face was flushed, and his neck was shiny with sweaty droplets trickling downwards. Herbert's eyes and face showed obvious frustration, and his hair was muffled from being tossed around.

"Do you need another break?" I asked. Herbert shook his head stubbornly. It was only at my insistence that we took breaks in the first place.

"I'm fine, Aylene," he said. "Just keep casting your damn spells." Bzzp.

That time, Herbert managed to mostly absorb my manabolt instead of redirecting it. This was a successful defense, but it was not the technique we were supposed to be practicing. Funny enough, Absorption is significantly more difficult... but that didn't make Professor Redsby any happier. The telling 'zeeboop' of an absorption gave him away.

"For crying out loud, Hardbub," said Professor Redsby. She turned to face us and her teeth were clenched with seething annoyance. She looked like she wanted to pull out either her hair, or his. "We are working on *Redirection*. Not *Inflection*, not *Absorption*, no, we're not working on *Amplification*. Redirection, Hardbub. Have I made myself clear?"

"As a Banshee's barrier," grumbled Herbert.

"Excuse me?" asked the High Mage.

Herbert cleared his throat and said again, "as a Banshee's barrier."

She looked furious. Her blue eyes were glowing bright like radiant sapphires. It looked like she wanted to impale him with an ice spike. A Banshee is the English adaption of a rather derogatory term usually directed at older magi women.

There is a myth we read in later childhood that uses that word to refer to a mage whose unpleasant personality led to her husband fleeing Atlantis on a whaling voyage in the pursuit of 'Gemcrust Humpbacks', note that you capitalize the names of magic creatures, out of respect. These were supposedly the size of a small village, before they were hunted to extinction. As the story goes, some twenty years later (observed through a binding curse she had placed on him in his sleep on their honeymoon), after three separate head injuries and a handful of lovers, the Alvish mage returned to his home city. He was eager to return to the wife he thought he had departed from only a year or so before. A cruel spell gave him an unpleasant death, and then she took her life, and then she chose to haunt other magi sailors.

"Get. Out," she seethed. "Both of you! Save me my time and don't bother returning to class until you've figured out how to properly use the ability you should have mastered last year. If you had one-twentieth the prowess of your father, perhaps I would regard your graduation as a plausible occurrence."

My mouth gaped open. I was shocked. "But Professor, I didn't…"

Wizzeep. I couldn't even finish my sentence before the High Mage warped us outside of the training room. She'd sent us all the way across campus to the middle of the fields behind the stadium and gym. I didn't even have a chance to be startled before my feet plopped down onto the grass.

"You idiot!" I shouted. "Why'd you say that to her? That was horrible. Did you *see* how mad she was?"

Herbert shrugged and smiled weakly. The professor and

pupil had a history, apparently. He didn't look frustrated any more, just exhausted. Exhausted and maybe a little bit relieved that he was no longer being scolded.

"Ugh. Whatever... let's just warp back to the Castle," I said.

An especially mocking ting, the tone of which wavered up and down, informed me that the High Mage had manalocked us.

"Heh. It's a bit of a trek back, isn't it?" said Herbert, scratching his head sheepishly.

I shook my hands at Herbert, exasperated. "God da- ... ugh! Whatever... let's just walk back."

Herbert looked at me funny, tilting his head to the side slightly. I don't know what happened or what he was looking at, but it seemed it helped him back to his normally cheerful self. I noticed a twinkle in his eyes, which were light brown, and the curls of his dirty-blond hair. His emerald and gold silk raiment were flowing slightly in the breeze.

"Off and away then," he said, twirling his finger into the air for emphasis. "Onwards we march!"

I rolled my eyes at him and pulled a hairband off of my wrist and put my hair into a pony tail. And so we began our first walk together, our first time together spent in private. It was the first of many corresponding class periods where it was apparently my duty to train with him. He was older, but I was better. More importantly, I had the patience necessary to train him, and the professor did not.

On the way back to main campus, we spoke, and I learned more about him and remembered things that I'd forgotten. His mother had been killed by Drakesh, one of Da'raakan's commanders. Herbert was in fact two years older than me, not three, and was a sophomore, but he was currently retaking Defensive Magic I. When we finally reached the Glass Castle, Herbert invited me to have lunch with him in his apartment. He lived in the most lavish of the dormitories on campus, reserved for Highborn. I was a little frazzled, and I declined, though my resistance to his friendly persistence would eventually subside.

"Come on…" he said, "you must be starving! I'll whip us up something marvellous. Surely you want to eat something better than what that dreadful dining hall has to offer?"

I frowned at him. "Not all of us were raised on steak, lobster… and truffles."

Herbert shrugged. "Suit yourself, but you're missing out. Anyways… how about we meet at class time near North Village on Friday?"

"Fine. The sooner we can get back to class the better. God knows how many lessons I'm going to miss out on because of you."

I turned away and told him that I'd see him later… perhaps a little more coldly than was necessary. He didn't say anything. I think I might've offended him a little. I felt his gaze on me as I left, making my way to my dorm. I'd only walked maybe twenty feet from him when he called my name.

"Candent!" he said, not yelling, not soft, but just loud enough for me to hear him clearly.

I turned and faced him. "What!"

"I don't blame you for what happened," he said, more solemn. "You were just a child."

I felt a familiar heaviness in my heart and put on a braver face than I felt. Herbert frowned, his brow furrowed. He looked a little worried in much the way I didn't need or care for. I was more than capable of taking care of myself. I did not need others worrying about me, and I certainly did not need pity. Still silent, I left. I turned away again from my friendly fellow, the handsome Herbert. Herbert who was so warm of disposition, and so seemingly inept in magical aptitudes, that we found ourselves in that predicament. I left and walked to my dorm, happy to find that my roommates were still at their various classes. I was happy that I would be left alone. I had the hope of a new friend.

Chapter 3

Bonfire

It was a night of early autumn sweetness. The air had hints of baked pumpkin pie and woody smoke, and the moon looked down at us through clear skies. The week had finished and I was hanging around, but not directly with, a lot of other freshmen. There were a bunch of benches all around a dorm tower, a bonfire pit near the centre of the area, and someone had set up a Bluetooth speaker. Upbeat music, laughter and smiles, the boys were flirting with the girls, and the girls were acting a lot less interested than I think they really were.

The trees, and there were so many of them around campus, were the sunburst of magi fall. I was sitting beneath one tree, swinging back and forth on a conjured swing. Although I was quite a bit apart from the bonfire and the others, I could still feel the warmth of the breeze that passed over the flames. I was a little frustrated; it had been a long week at school, and trying to help Herbert catch up was really draining. On my own time, I'd been practicing the other spells listed on Redsby's syllabus. I didn't want to fall behind.

Sitting on my swing, rocking lightly, I tried not to think about class. I tried to watch and focus on the light and the flickering shadows cast by the flames. I liked seeing the way they landed on everyone, the way people's faces were lit up and darkened. I liked trying to read the lips as they spoke flirtations and the corresponding coyness. Bzzting! Everyone looked to face the warp sound and then cheered. Herbert Hardbub and several of his 'brothers' had materialized, dressed in matching festive garments: orange with black trim and golden buttons and gaudy golden cloaks. Between them was a large wooden chest, a reddish mahogany with rusted-to-green bronze ring handles.

Herbert stepped forward. "Freshmen! Of whom we are so very fond! The brothers of Lambda Tau Epsilon are proud to have brought to you upon this lovely evening an assortment of mmmm-erriments!"

Immediately afterwards, with rehearsed timing, one of Herbert's companions stepped forward. Unlike Herbert, he was wearing a jester hat and odd slippers, the tips of which pointed up in a swirl and dangled a golden bell. He looked absolutely ridiculous. Bartholomew, as I would later come to know his name, did a jig, and a twirl, and finished with a tapping dance. Each movement, for those brief seconds, with each tap of the foot came the bright ching of an Alvish bell. When he had finished, he stood still and raised his hands into the air with an inviting gesture.

"Come forth!" said Bartholomew. "And enjoyyyyy the bounty of delightful tastes granted upon thee by the brothers of Lambda Tau Epsilon!"

With the conclusion of his words came a roar of applause and whistles and arms thrust into the air by my freshmen peers, with (in my opinion) excessive enthusiasm. Even so, after watching them open the chest and hand out bottles, my curiosity was piqued. I disconjured my swing and warped closer to the many students.

A curious aspect of magi culture, that one ought to be aware of, is that there is a reasonable distance from others that one is expected to maintain when warping closer. Otherwise known as personal space, but for a proper warping, you're supposed to leave at least ten or so feet between the two of you. I followed such rules of polite society, having been educated in the courtesies as a child. I walked towards Herbert from a more-than-acceptably-polite distance. I cleared my throat. Herbert saw me and lit up like a candle.

"Candent!" he said. "And here I was thinking you'd be cozied up in the library or casting fireballs at statues."

I looked at him, incredulous. "Shouldn't *you* be the one practicing? You *do* know that I can't go back to class because of you...? Or did you forget?"

Herbert blushed and his friends nudged him with their elbows and shook their heads with half-genuine disappointment.

"Tsk-tsk, Hardbub," said Martin, another buffoon from Lambda Tau. "Look at you, neglecting your academic proficiencies and partaking in such exquisitries when you ought to be practicing with the missus."

I squinted at Martin, mouth open. "Herbert, who is this idiot?"

The frat brothers, Martin included, laughed. Still snickering, tapping himself on the chest, he replied, "Why, this idiot over here? Who could such a fellow be other than Martin of the House Von Bear!" Another Highborn. Wonderful.

Martin bowed to me, playful and exaggerated. "What an enchanted pleasure to make your acquaintance, my lady."

I wanted to stay annoyed with Herbert, I really did, but their grins, outfits, and Bartholomew in particular looked so ridiculous that it was just impossible to keep a straight face.

"Were I to offer a bottle of artisanal root beer," said Herbert, with a twinkle in his light brown eyes, "would a lovely lady such as yourself be inclined so as to accept my gesture?"

That one got a sceptical raising of the eyebrow. "Root beer? You're handing out *root beer?*"

Herbert smiled. "And pumpkin beer, both of the non-alcoholic variety. What sort of irresponsible hooligans do you suppose us to be? You're underage!"

Magi don't drink until we turn nineteen. I looked them up and down. "Haven't quite made up my mind on that one, yet. Fine."

Chest already open, Martin snapped his finger (for flourish, not out of magical necessity), and warped a bottle into his hand and offered it to me. I accepted it, examined it, and determined that it was in fact an unopened root beer. I twisted it open, pocketed the cap in my bronze training raiment, and thanked him. I sipped it. It was, I must reluctantly admit, astonishingly delicious. It had a complexity and richness of flavour which, combined with the sharp fizzle, tasted just about magical. There is a rather extensive arsenal of ingredients with properties of a magical nature that our gourmands have experimented with over the last two millennia in drinks ranging from soda's to potent magic elixirs.

Our sodas have been in production for many centuries, and they don't go flat, need preservatives, nor do they involve high fructose corn syrup. And so I stood with them and sipped, saying nothing but smiling because it was so delightfully sweet. I had a great time, standing around Herbert and watching as he and the Lambda Tau Epsilon brothers (lobsters, truffles and excess, in my opinion),handed out the bottled sodas and mingled with the other students. I was so much closer to the fire. Each pick-up of the breeze and I felt the waves of dry heat rush over us as we stood, as the other students chatted, laughed and meandered around the bonfire.

In hindsight it was such an odd thing, the way it all was, the way we all were, the way we were acting like nothing was happening. The way we were totally immersed in our bonfire night, seemingly oblivious of the war for which we were training. Flames kindled by becoming kindred spirits. We were not soldiers, then. Just children.

Chapter 4

Fury and the Flowers

Facts upon facts, myths upon myths, my magic history course was so much information it made my brain hurt. I'd never been much of a book person. I liked casting spells, not reading about them. Even so, despite my natural preferences, I had to learn the material - all of it. Professor Asenwesh had convinced me of that. How could we possibly master the most intricate of spells without knowing their origin, without comprehending the theories used to analyse how they function? And so there I was, procrastinating. It was towards the end of September, and the weather was pleasant. The sun still shined brightly, and the blueness of the sky was nearly absolute, save for the occasional lumpiness of a white giant.

How I loved the fields, the trees, and the abundance of flowers which flourished nearly year-round on our enchanted campus. I was training; my hair was in a ponytail, I had to keep it out of my face. Casting spells, jogging, periodic sprinting and then the amplification of Lightswift and the blurry moments of breath-taking speed. For a few seconds, and longer as you get better, your movements are like roaring wind. A layperson could barely even see you. You would just be a blurred streak of light, unless they were recording with a camera with a fast enough shutter speed. It's like every atom in your body decides it has had enough of all that gravity nonsense. There's really nothing like it.

The ancient scholars identified four base magic elements: Fire, Water, Wind and Earth. Fire and heat (and Frost, its near absence combined with Water... mind you, no magic can defy absolute zero). Wind, a nearly pure force magnified with the control of thermal currents as enabled by the control of heat through Fire Magic. And Earth is the stillness of lifeless stone, and Water is both liquid and the very nature of change and flow itself. Modern magi call that hogwash and have proven that, in truth, all magic is fundamentally interconnected. Note that, out of reverence for the different varieties of magic, the various kinds of Elemental Magic are capitalized.

Anyways, it is, they say, more accurate to think of magic as being an all-encompassing field of energy, and it is the directed intention and mana of the caster which funnels the energy in accordance with their specific purpose. The acoustic properties of specific syllables in a variety of languages correspond to notes which either individually, or in a rapid string of sequenced chords, form incantations. More importantly, perhaps, it must be understood that all magic obeys the same physical laws of nature as studied by the scientists of the laypeople.

Creating light is, well, creating light; that's probably the easiest manifestation of magic there is. Mana readily becomes light. Then you have things like Icespike, the pulling together of the moisture in the air and lowering the temperature, shaping the front into a spear-like point. All that, and in the same instant, converting pure mana into a force to blast it forward. A challenging but powerful technique, if you need to impale someone. If you are proficient with Fire Magic, you can heat up different sections of a 'field' of wind to create a pressure differential to greatly accelerate the spike. You can also create tornados, if you're a badass. At the time of my freshman year, precisely eleven magi throughout history had the documented ability to create a tornado, and only three of them could do so intentionally and on command. A titbit that would likely surprise and concern most laypeople is that the scholarly consensus within the magi community is that 'Tornado Alley' is the lingering result of magic-gone-wrong in an ancient civilization of 'Sky Alven'.

As I've already mentioned, incantations are sacred words the syllables of which you trace with your mind as you speak them. Most come from the ancient tongue of the Alvish or Alven, supposedly the descendants of the Anhelesh (archaic: "they who are like Angels"). Whether the words are Alvish, Draconic, or any of the other imbued languages, the words direct and shape your mana. Eventually, with enough practice, you can get past even saying the word at all. That makes it harder for opponents to anticipate and defend against your attacks.

Runes, otherwise known as glyphs, are more technical; we all study the fundamental premise, but it takes a very particular kind of mind to have any sort of proficiency with combining and adapting them. We memorized and learned to predict or sense the geometric matrix corresponding to an incantation. Runic Magic allows for the direct manipulation of these matrices, allowing for extremely sophisticated and difficult-to-predict magical techniques. Rings and octagons and circles and semi-circles and zig-zags and what-the-hells. You can also use mana to... etch (kind of like a scratched-in tattoo) a surface of some kind with the rune. You interweave into the shape the precise conditions by which the rune activates. When stepped on, when magic is casted nearby, when a specific spell is spoken. Anything you can think of. A conjured fire rune, pressure activated, the near-instant incineration of the unfortunate person or creature who steps on it. You could add trigger conditionals; maybe if the person in question has consumed an obscure variety of grape, as used in the 'Vineyard Assassination of 823'.

No thanks. I'll take two orders of Fireball and a side of Windblast, please. I'll leave the geometry (trigonometry included), paleolinguistics and the God-damn conditional if-then statements to the bookworms. I'll have me a good ol' Lightswift and a temporarily almost-metal fist to an unsuspecting face, a warp, ten warps, huzzah! You better watch out, Da'raakan. I'm coming for you. My name is Aylene Candent! Pronounced 'eye' as in to stare you down, 'lean' as in a nice slice of rare meat, 'can' as in in you're going to kick the can and 'dent' cuz' I'm going to put a dent in the skull of each and of every Dark Mage and Demon that crosses my path.

And so I trained, and trained, sometimes with Herbert... but mostly on my own.

My classmates ignored me, and I ignored them. I had more important things to worry about than being liked. We were in a war, the particular chapter of which had lasted centuries, since the Resurgence, and with each passing day came people dying.

Spells and facts consumed my mind, and my relief was the school's flower-dotted field, with her myriad of ever-chirping songbirds. I fed myself primarily on chicken, venison and lamb (medium rare or rarer when available), and vegetables, which I was usually unsuccessful in my attempts to force myself to eat. I'd always been a little fussy. I was at training halls early in the morning. I remember the precise touch of professors aligning one of my arms or hands to demonstrate the perfect form to amplify a particular spell. Verbal chastisement followed the incorrect mental pronunciations of already-known incantations, or corrections of the verbal utterances we were just learning and perfecting. Our manapools were increasing by the day. In my first semester I'd been assigned twenty-three books to read (not all cover to cover, but still). Restful sleep in my made-comfortable-by-tiredness bed… except for those exhausted nights that I zonked out at my desk, or in the Vault. I'd fall asleep in the Vault face down in one of the books that had lived in the library for so long that spent mana had given it a personality.

Of the four courses I was taking, the most difficult by far was 'An Introduction to Magical Utilities'. It involved the practicing of the everyone-knows spells and then elevating them to use advanced techniques. We all knew how to warp. The lazy among us had casted it since childhood to skip a flight of stairs. A double warp, warping two things at the same time, is about ten times harder. The tiniest mistake and you'll destroy both things. Forget about warping two people, even advanced mages can fail that task. Most are wise enough to never try. The fact that Professor Redsby can instantly teleport two people across campus, whilst simultaneously disabling our magical abilities, is a testament to her absolute mastery.

Swapping the approximate position of things was totally new. I wasn't quite sure how I'd even end up using that one, but it was a pain in the ass to learn. Same incantation as warping, but an external rather than internal focus, and two things at the same time. Then there was Conjuration. Conjuring a swing was easy enough… a seat and two ropes fused to a tree. No problem. A fully working bicycle? Seriously? That was our final project.

On day one, with a mischievous grin, Professor Vavato gave us the schematic detailing every bar, every gear, and we each received a pouch containing small samples of the various materials for us to study. We had to learn to spontaneously

41

conjure them in the exact form and positioning such that she could actually ride the bicycle around the training hall. We also had to keep it from dissipating for five minutes, and were expected to practice other increasingly difficult conjurations on our own time so as to prepare us.

A common misunderstanding is that the opposite of Creation is Destruction. Actually, the opposite of Creation in a formal magi sense is Dissipation. Creation is the conversion of energy into matter (a process only made efficient through specific incantations), or the conversion of energy into forces so as to *affect* already existing matter (be it the atoms in a single apple, or the atoms in a person's body). You can *create* a tiny point of heat as a source of ignition for, let's say, gunpowder. Creation is also called 'Conjuration' and the word is used in contexts such as when I conjured a swing. That involved creating equal lengths of rope (or a rope-like material, anyways; there are magic materials that are simpler to conjure than naturally-derived laypeople rope), alongside a comfortably-shaped bottom panel suitable for sitting. You could conjure a sticky residue to affix the ropes to the seat, and the ropes to a tree.

Dissipation is the fact that anything that has been conjured, as pure mana temporarily taking the form of a physical manifestation, will eventually decay back into ambient energy. You cannot create a sword that will last forever, because that would take infinite energy. Similarly, you cannot gain nourishment from conjured food. It just dissipates and you're as hungry and sans-nutrition as you were before eating, minus a bit of wasted energy for digesting zero-calorie food.

One of our early, difficult assignments in my magical utilities course was the creation of a ball-point pen. Sounds easy enough, but the parts are really small, and if you mess up, the ink can explode all over your raiment. This happened to Tobias, who as a freshman was also in this class, even if he was advanced enough in Projection to be doing independent research. His mishaps happened multiple times, and it was maybe the fourth or fifth try when he incinerated his desk in frustration. He must not have been paying attention during Professor Vavato's lecture.

She had very clearly recommended separately creating the tube, separately filling it with black ink, and then warping it into place with the plastic and metal parts. I could do all of that, but for some reason, I couldn't get the black ink right. I'd fill up the tube with the same material, I'd click the pen, and then I'd write on blank paper and nothing would come out. This baffled Vavato as well, as she evaluated the chemical composition and determined it to be identical.

Making bright light is easy. Suppressing light is harder and I couldn't quite seem to fully cast that incantation, though I was decent enough at reducing the intensity and changing the colour. Our class ended up moving onto Manacharge and Manaleech before I figured it out. Manapools naturally refill over time, with food and rest, but Manacharge lets you 'borrow' in a sense from your future self. More mana now, slower replenishment and more sleep later, but if you pushed yourself too hard you could damage your life force or accidentally die.

Manaleech, on the other hand, is the 'extraction' of mana from living things, from imbued or enchanted objects, and occasionally from the rare places where spent mana naturally accumulates. Having hosted mages for several hundred years, the Academy was one such place where spent mana naturally accumulated. It was kind of like a lingering radiation that covered the campus, but it was magic, and it was most concentrated in the training halls. The better you got at Manaleech the more you could pull and the faster you could pull it, but everyone needs to sleep eventually.

Tobias, as it turns out, had a particular aptitude for Manaleech. I remember the first time I saw him practice outside of class.

I was walking through part of the forest that surrounded our campus. It was still autumn but the Aeromages had reduced the temperatures around the main parts of campus. It took a lot of energy to keep the entire place pleasant. The further from the Glass Castle, the colder it got, but I liked the crispness of the wind in the forest. It was an enjoyable feeling; the cold air hitting your skin, then the warmth from your mana spreading outwards to keep you cosy. There was the beauty of the trees, the fresh earthiness to the air. There was the slight trickle of the small streams which flowed here and there on their final voyage before the frosty freeze of coming winter.

Suddenly, surprising me, I heard the telling 'scsss' of someone manaleeching. It was a really shrill sound, easy to notice, and it was odd because I spun around and looked and couldn't see anyone. And Manaleech was a spell that wasn't really loud enough to hear from far away in the first place. I decided to follow the sound and I ended up near the top of a small gully. Some river, from ages ago, had carved a deep pass through the rocky earth. The sound got louder as I approached it, and I went down the incline and across and then climbed up the other side. To my surprise, once on the other side, I spotted Tobias in the distance. Silk raiment of a conspicuous, easy-to-spot redness, his clothing shimmered like ruby fish scales. He had his palm open and was leeching from a huge tree. Even from my distance, I could see the greenish energy streaming towards and into his palm. A little rudely, I warped close to Tobias, quite obviously

44

past that courteous distance Highborn mages are taught that they ought to maintain.

"Good morning," said Tobias, turning to face me but not stopping. There was an odd sing-songiness to his voice.

I ignored his greeting. "Why are you leeching the tree?"

"Why do people drink water?" he said, turning back away from me. "I'm thirsty."

"There's an ocean of mana around main campus, there's no need to harass a tree," I said.

Tobias turned to face me and smiled. "The ocean is salty, you know. Have you ever leeched a tree?"

"Never had a need to. And I'm not that kind of person."

I stood there and glared at him, my hair fastened in the usual ponytail I wore it in while training. My arms were crossed and my face was scrunched into a deeply-annoyed scowl. Tobias looked totally and utterly indifferent to my annoyance.

"You should try it some time," said Tobias, chuckling as he brushed a lock of his dusty brown hair behind his ear. "It's much fresher, much more pure. There's no distortion and none of the bitter aftertaste of that pool of, excuse my frankness, recycled garbage."

"What the hell is wrong with you?" I asked, glaring at him, my eyes squinting with anger and just about twitching. "How would *you* feel if you were the tree?"

His eyes, unnervingly dark, stared into my reddish-amber. "Rather honoured, I would say."

Ignoring my request, which I perceived as a challenge, Tobias turned his back away from me and resumed his total focus on draining the tree to recharge himself. I zapped him with a manabolt. Tobias turned and faced me, frowning slightly, again staring into me and past me as though I were a barely-seen figure in the distant background.

"That was rather rude, Aylene," he said, his voice quiet but slightly annoyed. His voice descended to that deep tone of Draconic before his self-control brought it back to human.

"Would you have preferred that I leeched you?"

"That would also have been rude," he said, his full composure regained. "There are manners and ways expected of us... you of all people ought to know that."

"Just leave the tree alone and go back to main campus."

Tobias tilted his head, looking at me with a weird amusement. "Is there a particular manner by which you anticipate being able to force me to do so?"

I was about to speak, but before I could, Tobias deliberately descended his voice. He spoke unnervingly slowly. It was like the temporary deepness of his voice made my bones vibrate. "I would hope not, though. I think that such an attempt would be rather foolish of you."

I warped backwards a few feet and shifted to a battle stance, arms in front of me, right arm above my left. Left hand held closer to me, defensive position, my right arm stretched forward and my palm was open and facing Tobias. He, like Herbert, was a member of one of the formerly seven (now six) Great Houses, the Highborn, the mages of whom in general were renowned for their innate magical abilities. The semi-translucent shimmer around my left hand indicated a pre-casting of Barrier, but I didn't reveal to him what I'd do with my right.

In assuming the stance that I had, I had challenged Tobias to a duel, a duel the terms of which had not been explicitly outlined. In accordance with magi law, any and all magic cast by Tobias, save for Dark Magic, would be considered legally-permissible self-defence. Casually, with an almost indifferent flick of the

46

wrist, Tobias cast at me a snowball-sized fireball. No bigger than my fist, a calculated toss, he even slowed the speed down as if he intended for me to block it with ease. Scchhuup! I opened my barrier with a cast, it too also of a calculated size, just large enough to block and dissipate the swirling flame sphere he tossed towards me. Tobias smiled and rapid-casted three slightly-larger fireballs in a half-moment, each faster than the other. I blocked the first two and deflected the third back towards him. As if he had anticipated my movement, he spun around in a dance-like twirl. Another casual flick of the wrist deflected his third fireball up towards the cerulean autumn skies. He was toying with me. And that pissed me off.

I warped to the left, and then to right, back and forth. Each rephasing was accompanied by the imperceptible clear ball and the roaring whoosh of my windblasts. The first two were as fast as his Fireball casts. Tobias absorbed the first and blocked the second with that brief moment of a barrier. The third, however, connected like a solid-punch to the chest. I'd funnelled all of the pressure into a sort of spiralling cylinder and blasted him just above his sternum. He didn't flinch. Tobias furrowed his brow, squinting towards me, his dark and unreadable eyes staring into mine. Watching me, studying me, contemplating my intentions and his intentions and how it was he would proceed.

Both of his palms open, he parallel-casted two fireballs, larger still but certainly not hot or large enough for him to think I could not stop them. My barrier absorbed them, but it was too late. He had warped behind me and blasted me with a double-casted Manaleech, sapping my strength and surprising me, making me yelp as the hissing green bolt stung me. It was like having blood drawn with a thousand thin needles all at once. He had greatly accelerated his manarate, a sharp spike so that he could pull as much from me as he possibly could, in a single move, as if I were a blood balloon that had been popped and sucked up through a straw.

Tobias then double-casted Manabolt which shocked me with enough strength to make me yelp. It knocked the breath from me and pushed me back. I staggered and hunched over slightly, my knees bent and my eyes watering. I felt dizzy, but I forced myself to regain my focus and warped back into my battle stance, drawing on a small bit of inner strength. A tiny bit of my life force, to be precise. With each hand I attacked with rapid-casted windblasts, with a zealous a flurry to which he responded first with voidburst deflections and then with a reddish barrier. As he casted his barrier, I double-casted a strong windblast with all of my strength, and I separated the nitrogen and the oxygen in the blast. I ignited the oxygen and the fireball exploded around him. It couldn't harm him, since it was fire, but it would get my point across.

Tobias flipped his hair with a feminine flair and a cheeky smile. He was chuckling softly as he brushed a few speckles of ash from his partially-scorched raiment off of his face.

"You're a rather feisty one, aren't you?" said Tobias. "Fine, fine. I'll leave the trees alone for now, darling, if only to appease you."

I glared at him but he said nothing else, and then a reddish bubble surrounded Tobias. It wasn't the bzzting of a regular warp but the fiery crackle I would come to expect from him. And so he vanished, leaving me there in the forest, a little hazy, confused, totally drained from our encounter. Every now and then I'd feel aftershocks from his manabolt, sharp and painful flare-ups that made me yelp as I limped back towards my dorm at main campus. At least I recovered quickly.

Chapter 5

Lobster, Truffles, and Excess

The weekend after my encounter with Tobias, I met with Herbert in the evening for dinner at his apartment. He had, for several weeks, periodically and gently expressed a desire for such an occasion. The two of us frequently sat together for lunch on days where our schedules had overlapping free periods. We also had spent many, arguably too many, hours training together, if you want to call it that. I don't know why I had hesitated for so long. I guess there was just something more intimate about having dinner with him at his place. In any case, despite my initial hesitance, I found myself in his dorm, sitting on a stool in front of his granite countertop, watching as he prepared food for us.

I was wearing a dress, which I rarely did, a pastel yellow and it went just above my knees. Roman-esque sandals, my hair was fastened in a braid, but was also wavy. A few of the other girls that shared our common hall had convinced me to let them put make-up on, and make the traditional braids. I was very reluctant, very difficult. I had never been particularly fond of make-up. In either case, the other girls poked and prodded until I gave in to their insistence.

For whatever reason, it seemed I was becoming less unpopular. A lot of the nasty glances and hushed whispers had changed to more of a quiet, casual indifference. Occasionally, a few of my peers greeted me with a soft good morning, a smile and a wave. Maybe it was because they had seen, or heard, of how hard I'd been training. I had a need to redeem myself, and I had long ago vowed that I would do so, at the expense of my life if ever it need be.

We had a lunch routine for those days of overlap. There was Herbert and Martin Von Bear and many of the other brothers from Lambda. Martin's girlfriend Vanessa and I often teased them at lunch; we called them our truffles. I swear to God, you've never seen a group of men that eat so much. Most of them had gourmet lunches delivered to the cafeteria and their dorms from a magi-catering company, or went to a nearby layperson town. They ate massive amounts of food, three times as much as I could eat, maybe more. Even so, they ate with grace, with refined manners. Not once did I see any of them make a mess of themselves. They just feasted for a long time, as if it were an endurance sport.

Chop-chop-chop. Herbert's back was turned to me. He had a cutting board out and was dicing onions and slicing peppers and other vegetables. Something was simmering in a pot on the stove and I could smell a pleasant hint of smokiness mixed with a hint of exotic spicy. I remember what he was wearing; a button-down shirt, black and sleek, and khaki pants, and a dash of bright cologne that was an interesting half-way between masculine and feminine. Herbert might not have been an exceptional mage, but I had a fondness for him nonetheless. He was admittedly quite handsome and always seemed to be in a pleasant mood.

"So, I heard it on the grapevine that you and Tobias had a bit of a scuffle," said Herbert, turning to face me with a curious raising of the eyebrow.

I shrugged at him, my shoulders bare; my dress had thin straps and left them uncovered. Herbert had, rather sweetly and carefully, hung up my cardigan in his coat closet near the front door.

"Come on, Candent," he continued, "of all of the people on campus, you have a duel with Tobias Racond and have nothing to say about it?"

"He's a lot stronger than me," I said, frowning. "Total focus, total control. I've never seen anything like it, not at our age."

Herbert scratched his head. "But why'd you pick a fight with him in the first place?"

I sighed and looked at Herbert, my eyes meeting his gaze. "He was leeching a Sage Oak north of main campus... I had gone for a walk when I saw him."

Herbert shook his head. "Are you kidding me? A tree? Of all the issues we have to deal with and you want to get into a fight with Tobias over a tree?"

I shrugged.

"Aylene," said Herbert, his voice delicate, "have you ever studied Magical Botany?"

"Well, no," I admitted, a little confused by his question.

Herbert scrunched his face. "Under normal circumstances... maybe you'd have been in the right, debatably. Trees are trees, ya know? Of course, Sage Oaks are a special case. But... there's so much mana lingering around campus, it's actually uncomfortable for them. They soak it up like sponges."

"Oh."

"Yeah... it's kind of like milking a cow," said Herbert. "For the most part, plants rather like it. There are certain families of flowers that'll chirp with the right technique. I have a bit of a green thumb myself. Most of the Hardbubs do."

My reddish eyes were still looking back at him, meeting the soft brown of his gaze. He'd grown out his hair a little, that dirty-blond of his I liked. It was quite a bit longer than when I first saw him, and there was an appreciable ruffled-ness. I wanted to run my hands through his hair and add a little bit more ruffled-ness, maybe after he finished cooking for me.

My hands were in my lap. I blushed with a quick moment of embarrassment.

"Well then, I guess I owe him an apology."

Herbert did me the favour of changing the subject. We chatted casually as he resumed cooking. He told me about some of the things he'd seen with his father. Apparently, you get to see an awful lot of curious and terrifying things when you're the son of the Grand Magister. We spoke about of some of the people he'd met, some of the High Mages and the various Magisters and their offices of glass and marble. They had antique globes which depicted veiled military bases, sanctuaries, and contained cigars with runes on their wrappings which added flavour. A particularly memorable and horrifying anecdote was his description of a Lesser Demon.

Lesser Demons, as the name implies, are significantly smaller and less powerful than Greater Demons. Even so, Herbert's description had me envisioning something truly terrifying. Black and swirling bodies of dense shadow, flickering like flames, they had no eyes but just an empty socket where you'd think their eyes would be. Squat, they hobbled like crippled imps, two to four feet in height, but they could spring forward with their tiny legs like they were grasshoppers. They could be fifty feet away, turn, and stare into your soul with their empty black pits. And then just a moment later, they would be tearing open your throat with the shadowy thinness of their razor-sharp claws. Sometimes a horde of them would hold you down and flay you.

Another woman, perhaps, might have lost her appetite following such conversation. I, however, hadn't eaten since breakfast; I'd been so nervous. Herbert's food was excellent. I expected he would have an aptitude given his appetite, but even so I was very pleasantly surprised. He boiled homemade pasta made with Bajhan blue flour, and the sauce was like an Indian cousin of Alfredo which was creamy and curry-like, quite spicy. It was a remarkably accurate take on a desert dish my ancestral people in the Kandenthakan mountains in India had enjoyed at celebrations for centuries. It appeared he had taken notice of my particular dietary affinities as my specifically-assigned sections of sliced venison flirted between rare and perfectly charred.

Accompanying it, Herbert baked a loaf of bread with olives - Kalamata olives - and I liked them despite my preconceptions towards unusual vegetables, fruits or other plant-based anything. I'd been sipping at a glass of water, but I was tempted to ask for a glass when he poured himself white wine. We chatted amicably, but I was distracted by the spicy richness of the meal, and the scent of his cologne, and his smile. I opted rather brazenly to reach for his glass, and pilfer his wine, somewhat confident he would not mind my doing so. Butterflies in my stomach, I asked him if he would oblige my request to refill me, and we shared that glass as we finished.

Time passed as it does, faster in those moments you wished lasted longer. Herbert and I were watching television, sitting together on his couch. He sat closer than I anticipated and had taken the liberty of putting an arm around me. I had a confusing mix of feelings about that, at first; I remember jumping just the tiniest bit when I felt his hand's warmth on my skin. In any case, I tried to relax and I ended up finding it a rather pleasant thing. We were watching something on Netflix; a comedy about totally absurd workplace shenanigans. I laughed a lot but more of my attention was focused on the touch of his hand on my shoulder.

I turned and looked up at him. He was clean shaven, and I said his name softly, and placed my hand on his other arm. There was perhaps a bit of liquid brazenness from my having imbibed, and as he faced me, I pressed my fingertips against him for a half moment before tugging him and his shirt towards me. Lips and lips, I acted on that felicitous occasion to enjoy that initial running of my fingers through his hair, and his eventual weight against my form was a rather pleasant thing. I was pleased to discover a toned firmness in spite of the Hardbub epicurean proclivities. In any case, a good deal taller and broader of shoulder than myself, and no doubt much physically stronger, it would be an easy mistake to make to assume that his will was the dominant force. My hapless Hardbub, a boar of a known voracious appetite - it was doubtlessly a pleasant surprise for him to find that it would be the Lioness who would devour him.

To Herbert's great annoyance, and to my amusement, not interrupting our *introduction,* but more aptly adjourning the epilogue to our epilogue, Herbert's roommate opened the door. I warped to the bathroom and a moment later parallel warped an assortment of garments towards my alcove. It is on occasions such as this that such abilities are remarkably useful; for myself this was especially true. This is because Herbert was both 1, rather unskilled at warping objects individually, much less multiple simultaneously and 2, was of a diminished vitality given the arduous nature of successive ardent embraces. Herbert regained his decency from the waist down, pants on, and I, having deftly re-cloaked myself, kindly warped a few of his articles to the room that I *assumed* was his. Oops.

And so I met Marvin, another Hardbub; a small fellow,

54

shorter than myself. He was wearing a hoodie which looked like it ate him, a pair of jeans and white sneakers, and his head was topped with a beanie hat which featured a spaceship.

"Hey... Marvin. How ya doing, buddy?" Herbert asked rather sleepily, his voice annoyed. "I thought you were going to watch a movie at Lighthall tonight."

Marvin looked totally baffled. "Movie night ends at twelve. It's twelve thirteen."

I smiled and waved hello to Marvin. "Hi Marvin! Nice to meet you. I'm Aylene."

"Hi! Do you play Glyphwalkers?" he asked, his voice brimming with excitement. Herbert grimaced and I sent him a quick glare and smiled warmly at his cousin, whom I had previously learned from Herbert was on the autism spectrum.

I shook my head. "What's that? I think I've heard of it but I've never played before."

Marvin scrambled over to us and pulled out a deck holder from his pocket. He opened it and pulled out a stack of cards in magiplastic sleeves. With a joyous, boyish smile, he shuffled through the cards as he looked for one in particular.

"This one's the White Witch," he said, holding out a card for me to look at.

It had a silverish border and a picture which took up most of the card and featured a lady with a tall and pointy witch-esque hat, glowing white eyes, and a platinum dress. It had text below the picture and a couple of numbers and symbols which made me assume the game would be really confusing.

"Wow. She looks so mystical," I said, smiling. "Is that a good card? What does she do?"

Marvin looked like he was vibrating with excitement. "She's really, really strong! She heals all of your minions. Do you wanna

55

play with me?"

I turned and looked to Herbert who, of course, looked somewhat displeased. I nudged him with my elbow and told Marvin that we would love to play.

I looked at Herbert and smiled as I asked, "Have you played before? The artwork on the cards is so beautiful... I bet it's really fun."

Herbert was frowning and shook his head. Marvin looked totally betrayed, and I rather suspected that Herbert did, in fact, know how to play. Let it be known that the Hardbubs are a jovial people, not simply hearty of appetite but quite fond and talented in many manners of merriment. Competitive games included. For the next half hour or so, until it was nearly one, Marvin showed me how to play with a learning game and undos. The details of this game are not particularly important, in case you are worried that you may forget them. But a quick overview will perhaps give context to what would one day become a prescient metaphor.

The objective of Glyphwalkers is to get your opponent's health to zero. Each player has a special circular stone, the size of a thick slice through the middle of a baseball. It has eleven notches numbered zero to ten. A metal arrow-like thing started at the ten, and magic made it move down and around the circle as you took damage. Each deck had forty cards. You started with four, except for the player who went second, who got an extra card. Each turn you drew a card and added an additional gem to your gem pile, until you reached eight gems on turn eight. Each card had a gem cost, and at the end of your turn your gem pile replenished. The higher the gem cost of a card, in general, the more powerful. The rules of the game overall were pretty simple, but each card had different text which explained their specific effects.

After Marvin taught me with the demo game, I suggested that Herbert and I play a match. Unfortunately for Herbert, or so his face revealed, Marvin had two *identical* decks for just the occasion. He retrieved them from his room, which I only later realized was the one which was the recipient of warped clothing belonging to a different Hardbub. To Herbert's great annoyance (and again, my amusement), Marvin spent two minutes cycling through each deck card-by-card to prove his claim.

Until the end of my days, I will remember how our match ended; Marvin's maniacal laughter and the look of extreme frustration on Herbert's face. Herbert, with a solid lead, had destroyed Marvin and I's final minion, Cloud Phoenix. What he had not anticipated, however, was Resurrection. The Phoenix arose with the miniature swirling clouds, and as per the card's effect, it doubled in strength.

Marvin whispered for me to think carefully, and to look at the many cards I had to choose from. Correctly, I selected Ascension, which destroyed your minion and brought it back to life as a Light-type. That meant it could get past his fortress minion. A brief flash of light radiated from the mythical beast as it rematerialized, and its form became a flickering whitish-gold. Again, it doubled in strength, and the massive direct attack to Herbert ended our match and made his Lifestone emit a humorously tragic melody. I grinned at Herbert with a cocky grin as he glared at Marvin.

"What's the matter, Herbert?" I teased with a honeyed voice. "Has a glass of wine too many exhausted your vigour? *Surely* you have a better performance to offer than *that*."

Marvin shook his head towards Herbert, disappointed but also clearly amused. He was the one who was more often the recipient of mostly good-natured teasing, and he was quite eager to take part in this redirected effort aimed at his cousin.

"Okay, enough," said Herbert. "You've had your fun, Marvin. What else do you want?"

Marvin yawned with a sleepy smile. "I think I'm gonna go to bed. I'm tired. Good night!"

I yawned too and Herbert looked relieved that Marvin was on his way to the confines of his room. I stood up and smiled to Marvin and wished him goodnight as he packed up his cards and scurried to his room quite abruptly.

"It's getting rather late," I said, my gaze radiating towards Herbert. "I think societal propriety behooves of me to take my reluctant departure."

Herbert offered to escort me to my dorm. I shook my head and gave him another quick kiss. He walked me to the front door, handed me my cardigan, and stood in the doorway leaning on his arm. I stood there, looking at him and him at me. Both of us were quiet for that brief precluding moment. He parted his lips to break the silence, and I warped closer to him and placed a finger in front of his lips to shush him, and I kissed him a final time for that particular evening.

"I had a great time, Aylene," he said. "Perhaps, if you are so inclined, perhaps we could have another such evening some time."

"Glyphwalkers and all?" I asked, my eyes twinkling mischievously. "A proper fellow ought not leave a lady wanting! Perhaps next time you'll offer a better match, Mister Never-Played-Before."

Herbert shrugged. "Irrespective of the failed outcome of my efforts, I maintain that my attempt to uphold my dignity was of a noble nature."

We were speaking Ameragi English, the Highborn dialect

with magically-enhanced eloquence. It was a formal manner of speaking which we would often use in moments of affection. He blushed, I blushed, and then I slipped out from under him and went walking on my way. He must have been caught off his guard because he didn't say anything until I was a few strides down the corridor.

"Goodnight!" he said, with that warm grin of his, the smile I had developed an ever-growing fondness for.

Again, despite my wishes, I found myself speaking in great detail of this evening to a handful of the other ladies who shared my common hall.

Chapter 6

The Vanguards

It's one thing to cast spells at a still statue, it's another thing altogether to train with a fellow mage. Getting my ass kicked by Tobias was motivation enough for me to try to join the Vanguards. It was only for the elite amongst our student body. Monday, Wednesday and Sunday nights, eight to twelve... and we had to apply. There were twenty-two current members, six applicants other than myself, and only three of us prospectives were freshmen. Of course, I'd arrived unfashionably early, and the others already there were mostly club officers and a couple of returning members. The initial meeting took place outdoors on the grass of the campus stadium. It was pouring. P-o-u-r-i-n-g.

I found the three officers and other members standing there at the centre of the grass field. Each of them was projecting a faint barrier just above their head, holding them in perfect place, barriers of the exact size to push aside the drops of rain before they hit them. And me, with my umbrella, a rookie; to them, anyways. I had been taught as a child to not opt for magic convenience, as a form of reverence. I felt my cheeks flush with the red of embarrassment, and I let go of the umbrella, levitating it in place besides me so as to keep me dry as a sort of ambivalent compromise. Laypeople and the Highborn used umbrellas, but most magi relied on magic - so where did that leave me, with my relinquished title and old-world courtesies? An outcast to those who should have been my people.

Chloe was the club president. The gold insignias on her black raiment identified her as such. Her spiky hair, cut short, was golden, too. She was neither frowning nor smiling, just watching, but she emanated curiosity as I approached them. The president said nothing. Isaac introduced himself to me. He was second in command, he had long black hair (almost as long as mine), a goatee, and a relaxed smile. It was only later that I would learn of Oliver's name, the club secretary, whose face was obscured by darkness from the hood of his raiment.

Seven applicants. Most of the rest warped towards us. A few of the older students matched the officers with steadily-maintained barriers of their own. A couple paid no attention to the rain, to the droplets soaking their raiments. Madison, who I was quite surprised to see show up, used Ice Magic to turn the droplets to snow. And she used lightly flowing wind to blow the flurries away. Tobias, with his fondness for fiery exclamations, warped into sight with a flash of flame and sauntered over to us. The closer he walked the louder the rain drops sizzled as the heat of his aura evaporated each droplet into steam.

Acceptance to the Vanguards was granted based off of our performance in demonstration duels. Isaac informed us that victory did *not* guarantee admission, nor did defeat necessitate rejection. Chloe, a proficient user of Analytic Magic, assigned each of us a duelling partner based off our manarates and manapools. Joshua and Seymour, both upperclassmen. Tobias and Oliver, a freshman and an officer, a match-up which would have been ridiculous had Tobias been anyone other than a Racond. Hector and Linelle, both sophomores, and as it turns out, brother and sister. Aylene and… Madison. Oh. That's me!

61

I was distracted; my mind was elsewhere as I planned my battle strategy. It was the crackling sound of Lightning Magic which called my attention to the duelling pair: Joshua and Seymour. Both of Joshua's palms were open, each channelling a continuous stream of electricity. Magi call this parallel casting. Each stream was oscillating at different rates; I could barely perceive the difference in the chaotic jumping sparks, and Seymour was defending with two barriers.

Seymour switched to a full-body barrier with his left hand and used his free hand to rapid-cast six or seven fireballs straight upwards. They were held in place for half of a moment before they zoomed down towards Joshua. The light blue bubble of a manashield surrounded Joshua, and the fiery barrage was too fast for him to try deflecting or redirecting. Defending against the fireballs drained a lot of his energy. Extending your aura to project a full-body manashield is usually a last resort defense...what a noob. All that mana wasted on a lightning show and a barely-effective defense with what little remained of his mana. Seymour brought his wrists together, his fingers spread out, and finished the fight with a double-casted Manaleech. Joshua fell forward, collapsing onto his knees, barely able to hold himself up with his hands.

And then he puked.

As High Mage Redsby had mentioned in Defensive Magic I, the average fight between two magi lasts a minute and fifty-three seconds. Between students, it was usually a few minutes longer, if only because we were expected to not actually kill each other. That's a no-no. Restraint is equally important to strength, if not more so, as a wasted spell and the accompanying mana cost can mean the difference between life and death. In any case, when two people are blasting at each other with fire, lightning, and ice spikes as sharp as spears, someone tends to die. Or surrender or retreat, and they do so expediently.

Isaac warped over to Joshua and asked if he was alright - a kind gesture, though I suspect the surprise of a hand on his back contributed to his puking again. Yikes. Oliver chuckled, Collette sighed, and Isaac flipped off Oliver. The president cleared her throat and stated that, in place of Linelle and Hector, it would be Madison and I who would fight next. Oh... oh fuck. I gulped nervously. Bzzting! Madison warped backwards fifty feet just as I warped into position, re-orienting myself mid-warp to face her directly. The swirling glow of pre-casted barriers surrounded both of our hands, all four; we weren't going to make the same mistake as Joshua. Collette asked us if we were ready. We stated that we were.

"Then begin," said the club president.

Madison tested the waters with an ice spike no thicker than a quarter, no longer than a butter knife, sharp as death. My calculated blast of wind pushed it from the side; changing the trajectory, it zoomed past me a few feet to the right. Bzzp. I jolted her with a smidgeon of mana. The silver sheen of a barrier spread from one of her hands, and she readied another ice spike with her other. I opened a barrier to match her, zapped her again, and then closed my barrier to parallel cast a volley of manabolts. She blocked six, the purple sparks of my mana dissipated against her shield, but two of them connected and jolted her. It wasn't really hurting her, but it was pissing her off, and that throws people off their game.

Additional ice spikes were met with additional wind deflections and the occasional well-timed Voidburst. I liked seeing the puffy mist and the icy shrapnel flying everywhere. Even from the distance between us I saw the glowing annoyance in her light blue eyes and the scowl on her face. She didn't hate me, but damn did she want to beat me.

Surprising all of us, a sphere of ice surrounded Madison as she whispered words. For a moment she was fully-shielded. The ice around her dissipated into snowflakes which swirled around her in a vortex of wind. She had conjured armour made of ice around herself. She looked like a Frost Golem. Her armour was a bulky suit of ice cut at sharp angles. She was like a crystal turned human.

Madison warped right in front of me and I only barely dodged a fist of rock-hard ice that would have slammed me in the face. Fuck. She wasn't playing around. She liked Martial Magic too, apparently, the potent combination of physical prowess and magical abilities. Dodge, frosty punch, dodge. The Frost Mage spun around and kicked me in the chest with a foot as heavy and hard as a brick. Well, not exactly. She *thought* she did. Afterimage projects your image like a living hologram.

If you're good at it you can even give your projection the feeling of mass and texture. Madison kicked the illusion of me, and my afterimage yelped as she flew backwards and winced in pain. A bzzting came as she warped towards my afterimage and double-casted a blast of icy wind. Her attack was so cold it would have drained the mana of most mages our age just to resist being frozen. Little did she know that I had warped right behind her, and that as she tried to blast me, I had amplified my fist to be as hard as steel. The glowing energy around my arm and hand extended forward, stopping at a point of piercing yellowish-white. I slammed my hand forward and punched through her armour, piercing her shoulder from behind, and I blasted the essence of her being with a manabolt injected into her nervous system. Madison's armour shattered into a million icy shards, like glass thrown against a marble floor; icy bits which sizzled into cold mist against my aura which I had extended outwards to a manashield. Madison, stoic as her mother, barely grunted as my mana surged through her veins like electric venom.

"That's enough!" said Chloe, her voice amplified so we could hear her clearly from where she stood.

I warped away from Madison, so I was maybe thirty feet in front of her, facing her directly.

"Good fight," I said to my opponent, offering her the magi gesture of peace, a hand tilted sideways, fingers curled and the accompanying flash of a pleasant blue light.

Madison was holding her shoulder, which was covered in blood, though the wound was quickly healing and the blood was starting to recede back into her. She thanked me, though her response omitted the traditional gesture. Maybe she thought I was being too formal. It was just a demonstration fight, after all, not a tournament. I warped away again, re-joining the officers and the other prospectives, leaving at my point of warp an afterimage for just a moment. It faded as I reappeared. I was grinning like a maniac, such was my fondness for the rush of victory. Even Tobias looked a little impressed. I shrugged at him, and he flipped his dusty brown hair and laughed.

Oliver and Tobias were the next pair to fight. Master Racond and his golden blood, his absolute calmness of being, a pool of stillness below which something terrifying seemed to linger. And Oliver; I remember seeing his face for the first time, his stubble, his chimaera eyes. One violet, one brown, and he had a smirk that was just as self-assured as Tobias. They warped into position. Wispy flames, so faint you could barely see them, were the outline of Tobias' aura. The droplets of steam fizzled even louder than before as they tried to reach him. Oliver just had his mini dome-like barrier above him, wicking away the water, his gaze locked on Tobias with unwavering focus. His right hand shimmered for a second as he conjured a sword, a dense material which looked like wood. He was going to smack a Dragon with a stick.

Tobias snorted with amusement. He clearly didn't think it likely that the swings would connect. Maybe he'd incinerate the blade. Or the swordsman. Collette announced the beginning of the fight. A fireball zoomed towards Oliver, and a pinkish swirl of energy surrounded his hand and converted the fire to mana fit for absorption. Absorption isn't easy, especially if you have a quick opponent, but it's certainly one of the most effective ways to win a duel. Why drain your battery when you can use your opponent's against them?

Summoning Magic is for most people rather difficult. As if it was effortless, Tobias waved his hands into the air with a whimsical flourish, speaking his Draconic words. Three Fire Elementals materialized and levitated a few inches above the ground. They were about as thin as skeletons, a bit shorter than me, and where humans have ears, they had horns of pure reddish-orange flame. Their bodies are flame incarnate. Magi bicker as to whether summoning Elemental Spirits constitutes using Blood Magic (punishable by death). Are they Demons... or are they simply the physical embodiment of elemental mana? I think some people are just jealous of the casters strong enough to summon.

Between the Fire Spirits and Tobias, there was so much rain turning to steam that all of us could barely see through the fog-like cloud. Tobias and the Elementals warped into position around Oliver and barraged him with fireballs. Oliver warped away before the flames had crossed half the distance between the two magi. He rematerialized behind Tobias and used Voidburst to obliterate an Elemental into oblivion whilst simultaneously swinging at Racond.

Tobias' aura hardened right where the blade would connect, and the sword clanged against the barrier. The bzzting of another warp and Oliver rematerialized in front of Tobias and swung again. They were blurred by the fog, but we could still see their shadowy outlines and hear the whoosh of the blade. Tobias extended a manashield outward and converted the barrier to flame and blasted Oliver back twenty feet or so. A bzzting and a funny glow and we heard the thunk of what turned out to be the wood-esque blade whacking the Dragon in the face. Tobias screamed, more so in rage than pain.

The two intact Fire Elementals were struggling to keep up with the two magi, tossing fireballs here and there in their fiery confusion. The roaring whoosh of a fireball blasted out towards where the officers and other students were standing. Madison's conjured ice barrier stopped one from hitting me in the face. Thank you, Madison. Chloe laughed and amplified her voice, telling Tobias that he should control his Elementals or else banish them. The dancing swordsman and the Raging Dragon. Tobias was an inferno; he sent out more fireballs than we could count. A few more almost hit us, and Tobias was struggling to dodge Oliver's swings. Each time he warped back, Oliver was on top of him in a half-second.

Not one to tolerate clumsiness, Chloe voidbursted the other two Fire Spirits as the rest of us watched incredulously. How deep was Tobias' manapool? For all of his being smacked like a rag doll, for all of his screams of frustration, he was blasting fire in every direction as if it was effortless. I couldn't have cast a fifth as much as what he had already casted. And that wasn't even counting all of Tobias' warps and his amplifications and manashields to soften the blows from the blade. Chloewhistled and Oliver warped back over to us before Tobias even knew what was happening. Tobias joined us after a blind volley of fireballs in various directions, and he warped back with obvious fury. Oliver was smirking. There was a cocky twinkle in his two heterochromatic eyes, and he pulled his hood up to veil his face in darkness.

"I always wondered what it'd be like to hit a Racond," said Oliver, more than loud enough for all of us to hear.

Chloe facepalmed and told him to stop provoking Tobias. The rest of us watched nervously. Not a minute ago Tobias might as well have been trying to kill Oliver, and here he was mocking him. Master Racond muttered something unintelligible and warped away in an angry flash of fire. His flames lingered on the ground for minutes after he left. So there we were, the Vanguards, the returning members and the took-another-oath recruits. The elite amongst the Academy, with our 'untapped potential', we were future Demonslayers. If only we knew that we had birthed a Demon of our own.

Chapter 7

Literature and the Sapphire Sea

Deep inside the Vault, more than a little dishevelled, still sweaty from training with the Vanguards earlier, well, there I was. *Arguing with a God-damn book.* I was working on a woefully-procrastinated research paper for my history course. Each of us had been randomly assigned a topic. Mine was "Truth and Tall Tales". The Alvish; clever, winged tricksters that they were, with their unending sense of humour, they had a tendency to imbue their tomes with magical deceptions. You could ask them questions, so to speak, sort of like searching on the internet. Sometimes they told the truth, sometimes they answered in Alvish or spoke in riddles. Over time, as they absorbed mana from the world around them, from the fingers of their readers, they developed complex personalities. Wonderful.

The tome I became well-acquainted with had retitled itself as Fábulito, and it made it quite clear that I was to refer to it as such. It had, apparently, spent a few decades with the companionship of a Cuban scholar. How it ended up in Massachusetts I wasn't quite sure, though I suppose I could have asked. In any case, on precisely four occasions, I made the mistake of answering a fellow student enquiring of the book's title. Each time the damn book corrected me, zapping me with a little hint of mana. This vengeance was often extended later in opportune times, with a good nipping of my fingers as I attempted to study.

We disagreed on a few matters. For one, Fábulito thought that I asked far too many questions, and that I ought to be reading instead. I, on the other hand, thought it rather odd that a book was chastising the reader. I suggested that it was lucky that I picked it up at all. Fábulito was grey with dusty neglect when I found it. I brushed off the dust and wiped it clean with a hand towel soaked in conjured rubbing alcohol. Good as new!

Especially annoying was the first time that I was dumb enough to get changed with the book on my desk, as I considered myself alone in the room. No eyes as far as I could tell, and yet Fábulito still knew that I was undressed. The book found a humour in whistling and the cheeky delivering of a few comments regarding aspects of my physique. I shrieked, thinking someone had snuck into my room, and when I realized what had happened… I was furious.

The next few study sessions involved sitting quite close and cosy besides the fireplace in my common hall. How *comfortable* the sofa was. I could just about feel the book squirm anxiously. Unfortunately, I had informed my professor of my chosen text just two days after first getting the assignment sheet, so I was stuck with it. A suitable punishment for my initial proactiveness which would later give way to the procrastination so definitive of the college experience.

Leaving the assignment sheet next to it was another particularly stupid thing because one of the things "attained" tomes can do is detect and contemplate the text on nearby papers. Accordingly, Fábulito was quite aware of its importance, and quite frequently attempted to use this as leverage against me. It thought that I ought to stop being coy and that a book as wonderful as it deserved the casual pleasure of enjoying the aesthetics of the human form.

I thought it ought to be thankful that I had cooled my temper enough to stop myself from supplementing the firewood in the common hall. The agreement we ended up reaching was, when not in use, I would leave it in a *very particular* spot. A few days of observation had supplied enough information for Fábulito to determine which corner of the room my roommates usually changed in. Seeing as I was not particularly fond of Elizabeth and Samantha, and in consideration of the word-for-word and in-their-voice recitations of particularly nasty things they said about me, I thought this to be an acceptable compromise.

Irrespective of our agreement, Fábulito was still rather displeased with my tendency to ask more questions than actually read. The comments and quips just about made me want to pull my hair out. As chatty and predisposed to gossip as Elizabeth and Samantha were, I usually read in the Vault, as I did that day. I was quite startled when Marvin tapped me on the shoulder. Comic-book-hero beanie, the much too large sweatshirt, the friendly smile and the vibrating excitement he gave off when he thought someone was about to play Glyphwalkers with him. I informed him that I was sort of busy studying, though in truth I was a little too exasperated to properly focus. Marvin told me that he too was heading off into a book, and asked me if I might like to come with him.

I was quite confused and tilted my head and asked, "You mean read it with you...?"

I hated reading my assigned texts. There was no way I was going to spend a minute reading someone else's. Marvin shook his head and smiled.

"Haven't you heard of Somnumes?" asked Marvin, confused

at my confusion. The word sounded vaguely familiar. I think Professor Asenwesh had mentioned them in passing.

Marvin gasped with delight and begged for me to come with him. I felt a little apprehensive, but decided to go along with it, and I packed up my things. In my haste I closed **Fábulito** a little more abruptly than it cared for (it got me back the next day with a painful nipping), and went with Marvin. I followed Marvin and we descended further down the Vault. We went down as he led me towards a room which had granite altars spread around the perimeter.

We approached one. It was engraved with strange runes and glyphs I recognized as Alvish. It had grooves and curves, like a Greco-Roman pillar. Its base and top were the shape of a square. Its height reached just past my waist and the top had a border which was embedded with gems of white and black. Diamonds and onyx. Marvin turned to me and asked if I was ready. I wasn't sure that I was. He opened his backpack and pulled out a book (a Somnume) and placed it atop the altar. The alter and the book began humming faintly, like a soft vibration, and then the gems started glowing in slow pulses. The pulsing grew faster, faster, the humming grew louder, and then the book flipped open to pages yellowed and crinkled with age and use.

Marvin placed his hand on the book and dissipated, the outline of his body shimmering with golden light until he was nowhere to be seen. Well. Here goes nothing, I said to myself, before placing my hand on the book. Vibration. I was the vibration. Faster. Faster. Too fast. Louder. The humming wasn't a humming anymore; it was a roar. It was the whooshing of tempest winds. It was the guttural groans of a Moss Giant. Light as bright as the Lunaris Twin Stars at midday. I felt my body warp. I went to a somewhere else, I warped to a somewhen else, to a dream inscribed in a Somnume in an age forgotten.

The cheerful singing of violins, or an instrument that sounded an awful lot like them; a duet of bright notes which celebrated an ocean unknown. The bum-bums of what I imagined was a Giant's drum. The fluttering of something harp-like and the windy whistle of the half-sister of a flute, soulful and sweet, delightfully reciting a joyous melody. The ocean. I heard the ocean in the inspired song even before my eyes opened and I saw it, as I found myself standing towards the front of a white wooden ship. My hair was blowing with the breeze which smelled not salty, but sweet. It was the mystic aroma which filled the air of the Sapphire Sea.

I was utterly astonished. A-hoy! It was Marvin's voice calling out to me from behind me. I turned around and saw him standing atop one of the ship's beams, one of his arms was wrapped around the wooden column. His face was the same, but his clothes were completely different. He was wearing a sky-blue tunic and brown pants with darker blue trim and a buckled-belt. He wasn't the only one there, either. I counted eight others, standing at various parts of the ship; some on the deck, some at the helm near the rudder at the back of the ship.

Alvish. They were Alvish! Their faces had the complex tattoos of golden ink which I'd heard tales of since childhood. Their backs had folded wings. Their skin glowed with the grace of God. In their faces, in their eyes, for a moment you looked into them and saw pure light, and then you noticed the perfect symmetry of their features. Their eyes looked into you, then past you, and they all had this same mysterious expression, the slightest of smiles. They radiated a joy as if they knew something you didn't. Something beautiful.

I tried to warp up towards Marvin but was unable to do so. One of the Alvish women laughed warmly, but the rest ignored me, and Marvin gestured for me to go over and join him. I walked over and then climbed up the ladder to the beam which Marvin was clinging to. Two wing-like sails were fastened to the beam.

As I stood next to Marvin, and started gazing at the horizon and feeling more comfortable, something shifted. The glowing beings walked around, talking to each other. Their voices were like the soft music. Their movements were blurred, as if they were in a television show on fast-forward. The waves and clouds that rushed past us matched their pace. It could have been a moment, or an eternity. I felt as if I had been there only a few minutes and then the sun was setting.

The blue skies faded and merged with the open-ocean sunset, and the music grew louder and a dozen or so Alvish joined the others on the deck. They danced, they flowed like palm fronds in what was not a breeze, but hearty gusts. The women had hair of a divine platinum, and were barefoot. Their movements had a hummingbird gentleness. It was a watercolour painting in slow motion, and they called me towards them. I joined them. I twirled like them, I was the wind with them, I glowed like them, my hair went silverish-white like them.

Chapter 8

Solidarity and Sorrow

It was a Friday's dawn. I had walked up to the courtyard at the top of the Vault. The sun was still rising and the horizon was the twilight of night-ending purple traced by rising orange. Across the sky stretched rows of bands of wispy clouds; on other days, perhaps, they would have calmed me. Today, though, this early morning before any of my roommates or hallmates had risen, I found the sight of them unnerving. I didn't like the silence of the morning that I usually treasured. No, that morning I stood and leaned against the bronze rail which adorned the perimeter of the courtyard above the Vault.

My heart held a dread that was such that I later found myself praying in the school's temple. Like most magi temples it was dedicated to the Divine Mother of mercy and prosperity, and her consort Father Justice. Hands clasped, my eyes closed, I was mouthing soft words. Since my father passed, when I was still a young girl, I had come to rely on my faith. Prayer often brought me comfort in times when I needed it most. Sometimes I spoke briefly, sometimes slowly, sometimes I was frantic, frightened and rambling. What words could describe the horror I had felt, and was still feeling? No words. Just dread. My heart thumped slowly as if it itself was too nervous to beat faster, as if the extra motion would make it burst like a popped balloon.

As I rose, walking down the hall of the chapel, I turned and looked up at one of the stained-glass windows. It featured Saint Helen, a white blade in her hand. She was wielding it such that it was tilted in front of her diagonally. One hand firmly grasped the hilt with fiery confidence. In her other arm she cradled an infant boy with open and curious eyes, giggling, blissfully oblivious to the warlike scene and his guardian angel. She nestled him against her chest, guarding him like a ferocious tigress mother. Her silverish hair gleamed as the glory of dawn illuminated the glass.

In here, surrounded by the saints, the warriors, the magi, I knew I was safe. I knew it, logically, and by the grace of their light which shined through the windows, I felt it. I was surrounded by hundreds of heroes of every kind, from squires and knights, to Saints and Spellcasters. Upon closer inspection, there were antagonists too. Casters of various manners of sacrilegious magic identified by swirls of violet, the base colour which most frequently connotes evil in magi artwork.

I went to the dining hall for breakfast. I walked into the room and a handful of students turned and stared at me for a few seconds, but then abruptly turned away. Something was off; I could feel it. There was none of the usual pleasant chatter, there were no shenanigans nor laughter. There were soft mutterings, solemn whispers and awkward and uncomfortable pauses. A professor came into the cafeteria and amplified her voice, and informed those of us in the room of an emergency broadcast. She conjured a large screen and tapped a button on her wrist guard panel.

Some of the students had already found out. A group of Dark Magi had successfully infiltrated one of our forward bases outside Rift 7 near the Mokroxi Mountains. The Voidlord they brought with them self-detonated, and thirty-nine mages had been killed in the void singularity or void bomb. Fifty-eight were seriously injured, and seven were unaccounted for. We had captured some of their ranks, but they had taken people of our own. It was a catastrophe; it was the worst thing that had happened to our people in years. The Academy, as an educational institution for the military elite, had a student body which had been disproportionately affected.

"Herbert, I want your opinion on something, your honest opinion," I said to my boyfriend. He and I were sitting in his living room, discussing what had happened.

"I imagine you are likely contemplating the wake services tomorrow," said Herbert, his voice steady. He was sitting calmly, sipping Rosesong Tea.

I nodded and looked at him; there was a truly worrisome paleness to his face. As the son of the Grand Magister, Herbert had met and knew well many of the magi who had been killed or wounded. His dad had hosted high society and the military and government elite throughout much of his childhood, even before he was Grand Magister. I don't know how Herbert was keeping it together; but he was my boulder.

"… I don't know what to do. I want to pay my respect at the services, but I have also been thinking that my presence may not be well-received."

Herbert put down his mug and held my hand, and squeezed it gently. I had gone from stoic to something between tearing up and crying in the time it took me to finish my brief words to him. He pulled out a grey handkerchief from his suit raiment and handed it to me. I wiped my eyes and blew my nose and started sobbing. I had tried to hold it in, but even the crest on his cloth reminded me of my family, and our sin, and our sorrow. A day of my childhood the occurrences of which resulted in my family's banishment, and the execution of my father.

"Ay, I have conferred with Father, and he and the other members of the Wing Council," said Herbert, "and in accordance with the decree as written, *you* were not banished. You were too young; and you are definitely going to see Lunaris before Yesteryear. I say this and hope this brings you comfort, and that it offsets my being candid with you, my love, when I say that tomorrow would be a less welcoming of days."

I nodded and wiped my eyes, and rose to wash my face in his bathroom. Herbert had to make a lot of phone calls, and I left to get myself fresh air and calm my nerves. It ended up being that class was cancelled for two weeks. Most of the student body had left campus and would be spending several days with close family members. Even after that, we were granted days of mourning before we would resume.

Enough students showed up to some classrooms anyways that their professors delivered optional lessons. There were many of us who felt a fiery hate that matched or exceeded our sorrow; our purpose was vitalized by the danger we knew we faced. The danger our families faced. Our friends. The billions of laypeople who knew nothing of the war by which their fate would be determined. We would have our sleep in death, our resting night, and now we trained and fought as the bastion shield of the light of day.

Dampened spirits, colder faces, more frigid hearts. Frigid not like Frost Magic, but lamenting loss. There was a deluge, fast and thunderous, that hung over our campus ground. The omnipresent clouds of storm lingered, the efforts and sentiments of the Aeromagi had no positive effect. As a matter of fact, it was highly probable that their pain had made the depressed rain worse. And understandably so; it was a nightmare, it was a catastrophe, it was a calamity. It was also not yet known how the circumstances of the attack arose; the investigation was ongoing and being conducted with the highest level of urgency.

It was a dark time during which I was thankful for the solace of warmth I found in Herbert, as he was for the warmth in me. We understood each other more because of that shared sorrow, and our additional shared evenings, some with and some without Glyphwalkers. And so too did he steadily and quickly increase his occupancy in my heart. Despite my fondness for my gentle Herbert, we no longer trained together, which was probably for the better. I pushed him too hard, I think, and he had enough stress from school and his dealings with his father and magi society. Herbert was a reader, a speaker, warm of heart and grand of spirit. He had all of his father's character, and he was well-regarded both in the school and the military community. But he was more of a warrior with words than a menacing mage, and so Tobias and I sparred increasingly frequently in our efforts for excellence.

The relationship between Tobias and I had shifted too; in many ways he was Herbert's opposite. Herbert had a heart-warming way with words, but was nearly powerless at magic. And Tobias was, most of the time, the silence of ever-sharpening death. If there was any mage on campus who desired the power to bring absolute destruction to Da'raakan, it was him. These days, following my apology and our frequent practice together, he looked at me a little differently. He didn't stare past me anymore, as if there was nothing there, the way he looked towards other people. Not all of the time, anyways. Sometimes his eyes met mine and I would see something hard to describe. Not sorrow, more of a numbness, like he'd forgotten the words he wished to speak. I saw in him what frightened the others, but I did not fear him. I felt the sorrow I knew he denied himself from feeling.

Chapter 9

Don't Let Me Be Misunderstood

The Vanguards met thrice weekly. Seymour, Madison and I were the three prospectives that had been accepted. The officers kept us informed regarding the most recent developments in the war. Chloe, Isaac, and Oliver had access to knowledge that other students didn't. As a team, as a squadron of the elite and the elite in-training, we discussed ethics and morality. When is it okay to take a life? Is torture ever necessary, and if so, when? What does a mage do when a magic act or magic creature is witnessed by a layperson? When do we report it, and when do we take memory wipes into our own hands? More frightening was the talk of the Blood Magic and Shadow Magic that we needed to expect our enemies to try to kill us with. Oliver showed us pictures procured from military reports.

A woman's face, greyish. Death had taken colour from her cheeks. Her face was intact but stained by splotches of blood, and the ground beneath her skull was a pool of dark red. Halfway down her neck and you saw the ripped flesh, what remained from the explosion. And where her torso should have been there was a mess of smouldering bone and flesh, the result of whichever incantation had obliterated the poor woman. Madison and I looked at each other and gulped nervously. Oliver just watched us with those two different-coloured eyes, one violet, one brown.

Martial Magic was Oliver's speciality and he took charge of mentoring Madison and I. He taught us techniques that we were instructed to practice on our own time. He praised me for my usage of Afterimage, but warned me of how draining it can be, and he was right. That was a last-resort spell, or a finisher. Don't give away your tricks before you need to.

Phaseshift was new to me. For just a moment, you go from solid to ethereal. Like when you warp, but instead of teleporting, you hold yourself in your energy form to let an enemy's spell pass through you. Timed poorly in a real combat situation, Phaseshift could mean a serious injury or even death. But mastering it could save enough mana to save your life. We practiced with manabolts, if they hit you mid-phaseshift, it was basically like getting tasered.

Madison was my match and more; her previous defeat had, if anything, made her push herself to surpass me. She took training to another level. I rehearsed incantations and did workouts every day; she did them multiple times daily. And that was before our first encounter. She had gone into overdrive ever since. I saw her training in the early morning, when I went on walks, and I saw her training after class. Sometimes I saw her in the late hours of night (early hours of morning… it's all perspective, really). With a flushed face and a bit of revitalization on account of Herbert's company and intimate embrace, I would opt to get food before additional training. On many such occasions, I would then encounter Madison, who was already at the training hall.

"How'd you get so good with Ice Magic?" I asked, mid-phaseshift, as Madison unleashed a volley of frostbolts (not Icespike, that would be a little too dangerous) towards me.

Outside of class, outside of answering the questions posed

by professors (and officers), she wasn't one to talk much. She was always a little standoffish, a little cold (ha-ha). I figured I'd try and change that.

"I learned from my mother," said Madison. "She's a Frost Mage, oath included."

Magi ordinarily just refer to themselves as being a mage (singular) or magi (plural). Any mage could technically become proficient with various elemental casts and other varieties of magic. Sages and High Sages being an exception of course, as healers. To be a Sage meant taking the Oath of Benevolence, to mark one's body with that sacred ink. It was the signing of a contract with the divine to dedicate all of your mind, body, and spirit to the act of healing.

"What oath?" I asked. I was not deeply familiar with elemental oaths at the time.

"She signed the Oath of Ice," said Madison, matter-of-factly.

There are, apparently, Ice Guardians. Or angelic-esque beings that happen to be dedicated to, or symbolic of, ice. Kind of odd, huh? Maybe it was placebo, superstition passed down from the Age of Lore. I don't know. The oath crests were certainly real, the circles intertwined with geometric shapes and Alvish letters so small you could barely even discern them. Seeing as an oath crest doesn't actually *prevent* you from casting other forms of magic, some magi believe that they don't do anything at all.

There was a certain grace to the way that Madison casted. She moved the way a wave of water might flow: smoothly forward, smoothly backward. The occasional sudden rush that also seemed to have a perfect balance. She might not have been as fast as me, but she had better aim. Each and every one of her casts was perfectly aligned to hit the dead centre of my chest.

And she was fantastic at Redirection! I'd cast a manabolt her way and Madison would reach one hand forward and the blue glow which emanated from the tips of her fingers would send my casts back towards me. When she phaseshifted she seemed to do it just as easily, as if it was effortless. Honestly, it was hard to believe that I'd beaten her when we first fought... she must have been nervous. She had a legacy born through her mother's glorious achievements; her rank was Voidslayer III.

Oliver told me in private that Madison's mother had earned the nickname Walking Blizzard. It was said that with a wave of her hand, and a whisper, her blue crests would glow and she could freeze you solid. And then you would shatter into a million icy pieces before you could even finish exhaling. You wouldn't even feel it. You'd just be there one moment and that was it; you were a cloud of snowflakes of blood and bone. Oliver and Chloe informed me that High Mage Nevien of the Arcane Guard wasn't typically assigned to the frontlines. She went behind them and brought frosty death to Greater Demons, and the occasional Voidlord.

It was towards the end of October that the real cold and bleak began. The clouds of unyielding grey bore with them incoming winter. The daily morning dew turned to consistent frost. The efforts of the Aeromages had, since the void bomb, been ineffective. That day, a Wednesday, I was having lunch with some of the other Vanguards. I sat closest to Madison and Oliver. The group of us were chatting casually, complaining about class, complaining about the weather, complaining about the long hours in the training halls. In all the lunch periods in the semester thus far, except for when we first met, I had not seen Tobias. But there he stood, with his black raiment with a golden trim and golden

Dragon-crested buttons. His face looked quite lonely.

"May I sit with you?" he asked of us.

None of us responded and there was an awkward pause. Even I didn't say anything, when I should have. It was Oliver who responded to him with a heartless disgust that I found abhorrent.

His two different-coloured eyes stared at Tobias. "Does it look as if we care to mingle with a murderer? With a snake, or a husband-to-be of a snake, more specifically."

Tobias said nothing. He looked to me, to see if I would say anything, but I didn't. I looked away.

"We only let you apply if but to humble you," continued Oliver with a snarl. "Go break bread with another murdered uncle."

Madison looked at Oliver, obviously repulsed, shaking her head. But she didn't say anything either. Tobias left and walked away, slowly. He threw his tray aside and I watched the rapid blaze and the ash that fell.

"Is it wise to treat him with such disdain?" asked Madison. "With such hatred? You weren't there. We don't know what happened."

"And yet you said nothing," said Oliver, brushing her aside with a flick of the wrist. "Not a thing. Should I count you then among the sceptics? Do you suppose that frigid mother of yours would give him warm regards?"

"You're being an asshole," I said, glaring at Oliver. "He's not the monster you make him out to be… you don't even know him."

He shrugged at me, as if to say, "Are you sure that you do?"

I picked up my backpack and took my tray and placed it onto the magically-propelled station which resembled a floating conveyor belt. I hurried over towards the exit where I saw Tobias leave through. I heard footsteps going up on the marble staircase and I rushed to catch up with him.

"Tobias," I said, reaching out and gently grasping the sleeve of his raiment.

Tobias turned and looked at me with a profound sadness. He mentioned that he found the reddish-amber of my eyes pleasing. He then asked if I looked through them, at him, with the same hatred. I told him, firmly, that I did not. I'd heard rumours about what had happened with his uncle… but I also knew that none of us were there… and who was I to judge, of all people?

I had the blood of one hundred and thirty-seven on my hands, and my family's title stripped, and all because my father was too weak to let me die.

I moved my hand from his sleeve, to his hand, and I held his hand and met his gaze. For just a moment I saw a blurred image, black and white, foggy; I saw a little boy with dusty-coloured hair sitting in a room set ablaze. I felt the cusp of the sensation, the particular psychic wound of having survived a murder attempt by a family member.

"I'm sorry," I said to him. I felt his sorrow. "I've heard people talk about it… but I never knew."

Tobias shrugged again, as if he felt apathetic, empty. But I knew that he didn't. I felt the just-beneath-the-surface pain, the heartache, and the justified rage.

"A Dragon burns if but by another Dragon's flame," said Tobias. "And a Lioness is shamed if but by the Lion's pride. We are two, and two, you know, uniquely disposed to comprehend one another's dread."

I held his hand a few moments longer. The two of us said nothing, and then I let go of Tobias and wiped off the wetness on

85

my cheeks. I felt quite sorry that I had not previously made an effort to actually know him. I just sought him for training as if he were a wall of Manastone.

I felt sorry for having challenged him in the woods way earlier in the year, even though I'd already apologised. We were both Highborn, or at the very least, he was what long ago I'd been. The Dragon smiled weakly at me. I asked Tobias if he had ever tried a Somnume. He told me no. And so I asked if, by chance, he would ever care to experience one with me. I told him that I would like his friendship. Tobias smiled, and I noticed the whiteness of his teeth, their perfect straightness, the sharpness of four Draconic fangs. I noticed the lightness of his frame. He was born of fire, to be sure, and yet I saw in him a gentleness.

"I would like that, too."

Chapter 10

The Flames I Saw

It was a beautiful mansion, centuries old. It was lavishly decorated in accordance with the tastes of gilded aristocracy. Sitting rooms, dining rooms, ball rooms, dozens of bedrooms, chandeliers of crystal, and fine upholstery fixed to each window. Oil paintings thought to be lost to the ages, unenchanted masterpieces that would have been at home in museums. Moving pictures will never be in accordance with the tastes and traditions of most Highborn, though we do wear enchanted garments on Yesteryear. How queer it must seem that the wealthiest amongst us clean our silverware with our own hands; we forego both machines and servants. Our magic gifts are reserved by tradition for moments of necessity. Seven families, seven crests, seven beasts; seven conquerors who offered themselves to the unknown in Lunaris and were then imbued with greatness.

The grey bleakness of the sky could be seen through the arched windows. Burning wood in a massive fireplace filled the room with a pleasant smoky scent, and appreciable warmth. At the centre of the room, sitting on a mosaic rug, was a boy. He was small, slender. It was difficult to tell his age; he could have been as young as six, or as old as nine or ten. There was a focus that seemed uncharacteristic of his size. Fair skin, rosy cheeks, long and wavy dusty-brown hair, neatly brushed. It reached just past his shoulders. It was Tobias.

He was the little boy, sitting there, immersed in his own world of fantasy. His plastic blocks fit together and made up his kingdom, his castle within his Dragon's den. He had plastic bins around him, each filled with pieces of different colours. He was sitting on his knees, alone in a house of silence save for the crackling flames and the sharp snap as he connected pieces. With perfect grace, he would turn and pull a piece, look it over, and then he would contemplate the shape and fitting he desired. Like clockwork ticking to a rhythm he alone heard, he added to his buildings or discarded the pieces back to the bins of the appropriate colour.

I walked closer to him and watched his boyish hands at work from above his shoulder. I saw the eclectic team of little yellow plastic figurines around whom his stories revolved. Their faces were simple, the standard print of ink they were manufactured with. But the torsos and weapons and armour were painted with the strokes of a slender brush. I picked up a piece; she was a queen, a queen adorned by a crown smaller than the tip of my finger. My touch confirmed her crown to be made of metal, and I wondered if it was actually gold. It probably was. Dragons are known for their affinity for steadily collecting artifacts, gems, tapestries, and other exotic lustres and lost-to-times. The little boy turned to me and smiled, and reached out for the queen, and I gave her back.

The smoke in the room went from pleasant to overwhelmingly thick. In an instant the scene I saw in his eyes went from childhood innocence to wrathful flames. Dragons, two men, roaring in Draconic; them with their blood gilded since before birth, since they were nourished by their mother's womb. Twin brothers, one of whom was Tobias' father. From rivalry since childhood, from resentment in adolescence, warring hearts were simmering; a conflict of succession. Their uncle's death, the head of the family, a funeral attended by hundreds, a subsequent duel, and another new widow. Another funeral, the attendance at which was suppressed by rational fear. An uncle who noticed hate in the eyes of who used to be his adoring nephew. His uncle knew all too well that Dragons can burn if but by another Dragon's flames. I know not who spoke the first incantation, for they were quite nearly simultaneous, but I saw whose eyes first held murderous intent. And in the aftermath, I saw the eyes of a broken victor.

Chapter 11

A Nightmare Disregarded

My heart was of the morning. Not sunrise but a few hours past. Skies of blue, I was the meadow too, and the flowers. There was a sweetness to the fresh air. There were pine trees in the far distance across the field. I was walking, in moments, and in others I drifted slowly as though I were a spirit blown by the wind. Back and forth, a few feet slowly forward, tugged by the air. Nudged to the left and to the right, and then a sudden swirl up and around. I was a leaf subject to the whims of the wind, and I was the wind by which I blew. And then I saw Tobias.

I tried to speak to him, but where words should have come, instead, was muddled water. There he was, in front of me, sitting on his knees, leaning slightly onto his side, looking up at me as I floated above him. His eyes met mine and I resolved, I was the wind no longer, I was a stranger no longer. His eyes were curious, and sad, and he tilted his head to the left. He watched me as if I were a strange thing in a land he found familiar.

I looked down and saw that I was wearing a silverish-white silk robe. I looked back at Tobias, and again I met his gaze, and then, for a moment, there was a flash of light as though the day had collided with itself. All white, all whiteness, no colours, just the floral and forest scent, chirping birds in the distance, and suddenly partially-translucent petals which flashed into sparkling existence. A million of them, times a million, falling slowly like wind-caressed feathers.

Warmth, I saw Herbert's smile. Tobias saw him too. Herbert's face was felt as much as seen. I gazed into his light brown eyes. His dirty-blond hair had earthly browns as rich as its gold tones. It was like I was reaching out to him through a mirror. The wind of light that was Tobias rippled, as if in understanding, with curious observance. I saw my mother, her smiling face, wrinkled beyond her years, and her hair was long and greyed. It was braided as always it was, her eyes were warm but sad as always they were. Her lips mouthed affectionate words. She was proud of me. I heard my father's voice in the distance, like a fading-to-silence echo.

I felt tears well inside of me, and then I fell.

I was the charcoal sky and the frozen raindrops which smashed against burnt cobblestone. I was the coldness, I was the swirling black, I was a silence unspoken, and Tobias alone could hear me. My mother's face drifted back away from me, and the remnants of my father's voice had fully faded. I was alone, or we were. The grey despair was interrupted by a soul-splitting, searing red light. A bolt of lightning struck and briefly surged to crimson, then back to white. The sharp snap of thunder became a vibrating boom which lingered.

Once more I was a little girl, my hair braided by my mother. I was wearing a dress she'd bought for me. I was on my knees on the grey-plus-ash bricks. The sharpness of the jagged stone had pricked me, and small trickles of blood seeped into and faintly coloured the water. Tobias stood above me, but he too was a boy, no taller than me. His eyes of sadness looked into mine. He offered me his hand, and he pulled me up. I brushed tears off of my face. We looked up together as the lightning storm flashed and flashed, louder and louder, red to white, and white to red. The thunderous booms were deafening; it was the sky's cannon song.

It was coming.

Something awful, something truly awful, something the very thought of which terrified me more than anything I could ever imagine.

It was as if I could sense the very tip of it, as though my soul was brushing the very edge. It was as if I could from the touch alone feel an iceberg of deathly stone reaching down into an unending darkness. It was coming. It was here. I felt a face behind me; it was the sky behind me. I did not turn to meet the face, the gaze. I did not have the braveness.

Tobias couldn't bring himself to look up towards it either, to the emanating hate, to the embodied void which desired only absolute cessation. Dissipation of all, of everything, perpetual silence, the only recourse of a force driven by its own nothingness-seeking nature. Tobias clenched his teeth, and his hands, and his lips had a tremor as if he were a snarling Dragon. It was as if a beast would erupt from Tobias' body and wrap around and strangle the face behind me. Tobias looked into my eyes. His eyes were a swirling hate of gold and red and black. But it wasn't hate for me. Tobias spoke with a Dragon's voice, a deepness that would rival the thunder's fading remnants. His growls rumbled with a magically amplified loudness; pure wrath. I felt as much fear in my heart for Tobias as I did for the entity behind me. A nightmare disregarded.

Chapter 12

Where the Darkness Walks

It's too easy to lose yourself to dreaming. Somnumes were a pleasant escape from the unpleasant realities that I often faced on campus. My association with Tobias had caused a resurgence in animosity towards me, and towards him. Herbert isn't the controlling type, but he was definitely concerned, just like the Vanguards (except for Oliver, who simply despised Tobias, and despised my talking to him). Somnumes, Herbert warned me, were unhealthy; or at the very least often resulted in unhealthy usage. Just because you *can* trade a few real hours for days or weeks in another world, that doesn't mean you *should*, he told me.

The mind and spirit can only handle so much. But Herbert didn't tell me to stop, and even if he had, I don't think I would have listened. I'd always been stubborn. The defiance and the Pride of the Lion's heart, in accordance with my family's crest. And so it was that I found myself quite frequently experiencing Somnumes with Tobias. With his sharp mind, and his surprising fondness for adventure, I greatly enjoyed his company.

White snow-capped mountains, old world villages, quaint people in folksy outfits and Honeybell Fairies; princesses with rosy cheeks and pursuant knights with broad builds and charming smiles. Festivals with platters of pleasant biscuits and cheeses and ales and meads. Christmas in a bottle... well, a book, really. Sand dunes hundreds of feet tall, mirages in the desert, ill-tempered camels and trading caravans and a newfound and deep appreciation for the sight of water on the horizon.

Alvish of the forest, with their lavender purple eyes and greenish hair, with their leather ornamental armour, and their strange helmets. The women's helmets were adorned with engraved deer antlers, and the men's were decorated with the plumage of exotic winter birds. I'd never had anything as flavourful as the fish they smoked in their wooden boxes, nor anything so sweet and calming as their blueberry wine. Between the food and the sounds of the forest, the birds and their bear bone flutes, I was seduced, I was enchanted. I'll always remember when Tobias and I stood there on the rope bridges connecting their homes inside hollowed trees.

But all dreams end, and some nightmares never do.

A natural progression from our enjoyment of casual literary dreams was a curiosity regarding darkness. Umbrumes. Books of a rather rarer nature, for good reason. All of the Umbrumes at the Academy were in storage in various magically-sealed archives. Some were sealed in chambers with encoded glyphs which only a master could attempt solving. Some needed a key, a couple needed three or more keys, and others had weirdly-shaped slots which you presumably had to fill with objects. Tobias was, in particular, tempted by the prospect of knowledge of Blood Magic and Shadow Magic, and a couple other things about which I'd prefer to never speak. Naturally, I chastised him, though I didn't think it likely he would ever use such incantations. There is no harm in *reading* a grimoire, or *observing* Dark Magic in an Umbrume, he argued, just as watching a horror movie is quite different from committing murder.

In any case, I pushed him in other directions, and we settled upon one of the sections of sealed history. The one that had particularly piqued our interest was a room guarded by a large door of thick bronze engraved with words in the Darmish language. It didn't need a key, nor did it have any of the unusual slots. It also didn't have a set of coded glyphs that needed to be solved for it to open. It was just there. It wouldn't budge, there wasn't a door knob. It might as well have been a painted wall, except it was a metal that seemed to buzz with electricity when you touched it.

Darmish culture and technology was a field in which Marvin had worked with professors on research. I found that out when I asked him about the various kinds of sealed rooms in the library. The Darmer, Marvin taught me, were the race who originally invented Somnumes (although it was the Alvish who were the most prolific authors of the magically-encrypted stories therein). It was debated amongst Magistorians (history nerds for magical things) that the Darmer predated the Alvish, just as many scholars have the opposite opinion and believe it could only have been the Alvish who existed first, and that they created the Darmer.

The Darmer had been mostly lost to history, even more so in many ways than the Alvish from whom magi descended. More mysteries than consensus remained. It was undisputed that the Darmer's civilization was characterized by the extremely advanced usage of mathematics, engineering and Astromancy (also known as Astral Magic). We had found their Automatons, deactivated of course, seemingly impossible to turn back on. The little of their language we were able to decipher largely related to Aeromagic for weather manipulation. There was a conspicuous scarcity of Somnumes directly related to the Darmish societies. It was almost as if they had sought to be forgotten.

And so it was that a Racond and a Candent found themselves seeking first-hand knowledge of the Darmer our textbooks briefly alluded to. There was so little known of them.

It is a common misconception that the maternal feminine which exists within women precludes the possibility of ruthlessness. The rosy picturesque is sweeter than thoughts of scarlet nightshade wine.

I am quite ashamed to admit that I defied my inner instinct, my spirit's whispers. Maybe there is in fact a special part in all could-be-mother's hearts. But that doesn't mean we always listen. And so, I must ask for a forgiveness I do not deserve; may God and the Higher Lights pardon me my sins.

I manipulated Marvin with full knowledge of his child-like soul.

I had frequently spent time with him when I stayed with Herbert, and Marvin seemed to have a particular fondness for playing Glyphwalkers with me. A sweet voice, a twirling of my hair, my hand gently placed on Marvin's arm in opportune moments. I promised fifty, no, *a hundred*. I would play more matches with him in the coming months than he could even count. Pleading words of honey for Marvin to open the sealed room in the Vault. Tobias and I just wanted a look around; some curiosities need quenching. We were, of course, forbidden to leave the room with any of the books.

It was in the dead of night that the three of us descended to the floor on the Vault which had the sealed room we had chosen. The three of us went down the stairs separately, waiting a few minutes before the next one followed. We were relieved to find that the room was empty except for the sea of shelves and their myriad books and the enchanted nooks and crannies. Once at the door, Marvin instructed Tobias and I to stand back, and then he placed his hand on the faintly-buzzing engraved bronze. He whispered a word in Darmish which I would be foolish to repeat, lest you tread past a line of shadows as once I did. For just a moment, as the bronze faded to translucence and then disappeared, I heard the faintest sound of choral singing from somewhere far away.

We walked into the room, and as I stepped across the empty space where the wall had been, I felt that odd tingling you feel when you warp somewhere. It wasn't actually a room *in* the campus - it was a conjured portal *on* campus. We were, as a matter of fact, in a real Darmish archive. An archive that could only be accessed by a couple of Warpgates around the world.

The floor of the room was some kind of granite with gold borders, and the engraved bronze walls were made green by age. Recessions into the metal wall were the 'shelves' on which precisely thirty-nine books rested. They were only very rarely disturbed. Nine of them, if touched, were known to cause instant death. They were sealed with particularly nasty Shadow Magic and Blood Magic incantations, and nine magi had failed in dispelling their binding curses. Without correctly suppressing the curses, eleven caused blindness. Seven compelled you to speak babbled words in a delirium that lasted weeks or months, and three scarred you with recurring burns. Five appeared to be blank, but likely weren't, but no one knew if those volumes would ever be deciphered. The final four had been deciphered, unlocked forever. Each granted the looker short but relatively unpleasant glimpses into a world and people lost by time.

Tobias and I were fascinated. The books had a sinister beauty; there was both a similarity and a uniqueness to all of them. They had dark colours and intricate, fractalesque lace decorations. Some of the titles on the covers were in golden words in their foreign script, Darmish. The symbols that were so very strange to me were their letters. Marvin pointed out which books were which. To Marvin's horror, and my amusement, Tobias hovered his hand a fraction of an inch above one of the lethal books. Who but they who calmly brush death could ever truly wield it?

We looked around. Marvin told us little titbits about the fascinating culture that Magistorians had gleaned. And then the eyes of Tobias and I, at the same time, landed upon one book in particular. It had a sort of tug on me. It had a resonance which matched my own. It was one of the five which appeared to be blank. My eyes landed on it, and I felt a sort of whisper in my chest. I could tell that Tobias felt it too. I'll always remember what it looked like; the cover was a clear glass with obscuring swirls of black and white which formed two stars that orbited each other.

I winked at Tobias, and I walked over to Marvin, who was delightedly reciting random lore, and I squeezed his hand and exclaimed my gratitude. I tugged his arm, pulling him towards the exit playfully, and I thanked him. We would play a dozen matches as soon as we left the library. Tobias asked if we were ready to go. The book was behind his back, tucked inside his raiment. He hurried past us towards the exit portal. He was the first to cross, and Marvin and I followed but a moment later.

The softest gust, from a forever away, accelerated to a howling, shrieking wind that wrapped around me like a thorned tornado. Blinding light, so harsh so as to not be holy, but dark beyond darkness, annihilated the universe around us into dismembered particles. We were less than dust; we were less than atoms. I sensed and saw the afterimage of Tobias and Marvin, right next to me, and then they catapulted across pseudo-existence. Our positions were warping around in that confusing haze; our souls were in a place we shouldn't have gone to. I heard Marvin's yelping and whimpering; he was overtaken by that arcane agony. I was struggling to resist a hell of my own.

The bleeding wind did not dissipate. The sound was nearly all we could hear, but there we were again. We had gone from absolute nowhereness to a vaguely-defined void. Three pillars of reddish light lifted us, nudging us slightly here and there. I screamed out to Tobias and Marvin, but my words were muted. My first syllable came out, and then my voice was instantly suppressed. Tobias stood there in the blood-like light, saying nothing. His eyes were furious, and his snarling mouth was defiant. Marvin writhed, seized and shrieked in pain; his agony was not made silent.

And the Faceless was before us. We were enveloped in a void, and in front of us was a colossal face of a condensed paradox of void and voidlessness. I could feel my breath being pulled from me as I exhaled. I could feel the tendrils of dread which caressed each of my energized atoms, and my spirit's quintessence. It promised me unlimited power, or a misery unending. I could be the Eclipse, the final bell, or each fragment of my being would be impaled upon ethereal stalagmites.

There were two souls besides me, and all I had to do was choose.

The deep echoing of that voicelessness made my being vibrate: *"All you have to do is choose."*

It did not speak a language but instead broadcasted meaning that resonated inside my being like forced telepathy. *All I had to do was choose. All I had to do… all I have to do… choose.* It was madness beyond madness, it was suffering beyond suffering. It was an unpleasant and confusing infinity. *All I had to do was choose.* Or we would be there, condemned, forever. *Infinity times two, times two, just choose.*

From the innermost part of me a truth tingled: I had to offer Tobias. The dark voice whispered for me to do it, *and how could I refuse?* Tobias had an immeasurably greater darkness within him. Each of our souls had been laid as bare to each other as knitted dolls pulled into a single strand of yarn. I had a wolf in one hand, and in the other a wounded lamb. My lips parted to speak, but I stopped. My eyes were still closed as I tried to resist that agony, and then the wind faded to soundlessness.

It seemed as though Tobias had made his choice before me. I watched Marvin as if he were an inch away past smoke-grey glass. Every quark in every atom in his body was obliterated simultaneously. Marvin was a nuclear explosion times a repeating million. His soul and physical being pulsed back and forth between infinitesimal ashes and reconstitution as he endured a time loop. Marvin felt the unyielding heat radiated by the hydrogen fusing in the core of a star. Maniacal laughter, power overwhelming, Tobias' aura stretched around and filled the nothingness further than my spirit could sense. Maniacal laughter, from Tobias, and then from the voicelessness. And then I heard the final words.

Death incarnate spoke in a primal non-language, pulsed into my being: *"Sweet daughter… all you had to do… was choose."*

There is a realm wherein there are no joyous lights. On their eternal night, if you look up, amongst their myriad of stars, you see sister worlds of dread. Rusty reddish with green swirls, ebbing orange and yellow and red and green, strange planets of a toxic miasma of death. I could sense that there were around a dozen of them, each with bright neon storms flowing past each other across their surfaces. Beware their tempting gaze; anything longer than a glance and you start to feel the vibration. At the back of your mind, you sense the particular form of suffering that defines each dreadful placelessness. Stare too much longer and your presence shall be compelled to join the embodied realm of the lord of that particular Noc'raakan. The planets both belong to a Noc'raakan, and are the Noc'raakans themselves; a metaphysical paradox of death and dread.

I arrived there for the first time wearing a ragged robe of white, with my arms shackled by a chain of dark-greenish metal. I was on my knees at the centre of a large hexagon-shaped room. I saw no source of light, but the room was filled with a dim purple glow. In front of me were three beings, two of whom were wearing glossy black armour with strange patterns of narrow engravings through which molten lava seemed to be flowing. The other, apparently their leader, wore only jet-black robes. I couldn't see his face from under the shadows of his metal chain hood.

I could see its eyes, though. Eyes of unyielding blue flame. It was staring at me, talking to the grey-skinned beings beside it in a harsh language which repulsed me. Hearing it made my skin crawl. It filled me with dread. There was anti-musicality to the words they spoke. It walked closer to me, knelt down, and placed upon my cheek an uncomfortably hot hand with sharp claws at the end of otherwise slender fingers. I could distinctly feel each of the six sharp points, pressed into my skin. Any harder and I would have started bleeding. It twisted my head to the right, moved its face closer to mine, and stared into my left eye.

The being tapped the metal shackles that were binding me, and they dissipated. I pulled away and stood up. I jumped back into a defensive position, and my hands glowed that translucent white-silverish of my pre-casted barriers. And then they started laughing at me. The hooded one raised a single finger upwards and I felt my mana flicker off instantly as if I were a light switch. I put my fists up; if I was to be tortured, or killed, I would go out fighting. The two wearing armour warped out in a flash of blue and violet fire. The robed and hooded entity spread its hands outwards in an arc, and the walls around me disappeared.

And there I was, standing alone on grey sand in what looked to be a dune-filled desert. I saw that dreadful sky, and I screamed out into the night, asking where I was. Each of the voices, the lords of all those ghastly demonic realms, they spoke into the back of my mind simultaneously. Cosmic terror blended into one, and I heard "Noc'raakan". Over and over again, I heard that dreadful word.

I couldn't warp. I was terrified, and I tried to climb the grey sand dunes which towered hundreds of feet up and surrounded me in each direction. Each time I scrambled up, by the time I was a third or half-way up the sand, I was pushed back down. Different dunes, same thing, slightly different heights as if to mock me. Each time it was as if a single, massive God-sized finger just pushed me back into place. I was like an ant, to them. To it. They were a paradoxical fragmented oneness of entities of embodied void, infinite silence.

The gravity grew stronger. Each step forward felt as if I were dragging a boulder. It was pointless. Absolutely pointless. I collapsed onto my knees and looked up and saw the sky again, my eyes pulled forward to the haunting planets. It felt as if I had already enjoyed a lengthy visit to each and every one. The shackles that had previously choked my wrists reappeared. Somewhere far away, I sensed Marvin, and Tobias, and then the trace sensation of their two soul essences blasted a couple of infinities further away from me. *I could tell that they went in opposite directions from each other.* The invisible finger pushed me back from my sternum until I was flat on my back. My eyes closed in a hopeless attempt to reduce the sensation of what I could now distinctly tell was thirteen Noc'raakan.

They carved into the quintessence of my being an understanding: "Da'raakan is but my shortest finger, and you are Ours. Be assimilated."

Chapter 13

Cobalt Blue

In the centre of one of the main halls on campus, as dozens of students hurried to-and-fro, as professors mingled, Marvin and I materialized. Sunlight came through the stained-glass windows, and students shrieked as their eyes turned and they saw Mavin seizing next to me. His mouth was bubbling spit and blood which dribbled down his chin, onto his clothes, and his eyes were glazed over. I was shaking his shoulders and sobbing. I don't know who, but one of the professors warped next to me and grabbed my wrist. I felt electric fire, and then I fainted.

A silky softness, the comforting mixed scent of sweet blueberry and hints of something reminiscent of but not quite a lemon. Was it citrus? I think so, perhaps some magical variant, natural or created by the enchanted hands of a Magibotanist some time ago. Eyes still closed, I inhaled deeply and groaned at the sharp pain which ensued from the small motion of my breathing inwards. With that quick breath and the sharp pain came the feeling of a soreness throughout my body, from the crown of my skull to the tips of my toes.

I leaned forward, biting my lips, scooting back and supporting myself on my hands with my back against a pillow. Again, I deliberately inhaled the swirled scent of the blueberry and maybe-citrus. It filled my nostrils and surrounded my senses like a honeybee field of flowers and fruits. I opened my eyes, and for the second time in my life, I found myself in a hospital bed. The overwhelming brightness of the midday sun beamed through an opened window. Birds were chirping in the not-quite-a-distance, not far outside my window at all. I was a few floors up from the ground. I saw trees from my vantage point. There was only one kind of tree: tall and wide Wisdom Oaks. They were cousins of Sage Oaks and had whitish-blue bark with occasional lavender splotches, and semi-translucent leaves, inside of which I saw shimmering sparkles of blue and white and gold.

"Hello?" I called out, to no one in particular.

Berrooshhk. A Behemoth of smooth white stone materialized, its body formed of separate segments. They floated together in harmony, vaguely forming a humanoid figure, but with shoulders as wide as an office desk. Its head was a sphere as big as a pumpkin and it rotated atop its torso stone an uncountable number of revolutions per moment. Even so, despite the rotation, there were two arcane eyes where you would expect eyes to be, glowing and cobalt blue.

Naturally, I was quite alarmed. I tried to lean away from it, and it hulked towards me and raised its arm of levitating stones upwards. Fingers of mana appeared and brought the silverish blanket up and covered my body up to my shoulders. It was tucking me in, and it emitted a pleased sort of chirping sound which I would not have anticipated it to have been able to make. This too was rather alarming, and I wasn't quite sure of what to make of this strange… thing-like being… this being-like thing? I moved my hand up to brush a lock of hair behind my ear.

A brush materialized and floated in the air, and the stone creature made a sort of questioning beep, as if it was requesting permission to brush my hair. I shook my head, attempting to do so politely, and it responded with a perfectly content chirp. Its duty, apparently, was to ask, not to be offended at my refusal. The creature disappeared, and for just a minute or two, I was alone and quite perplexed. Two people warped into the room. The Grand Magister and the High Sage.

The Grand Magister had an amused grin on his face, and the High Sage depicted a complex mix of three emotions in roughly equal amounts: pleased at my being awake, annoyed by the presence of the Grand Magister, and deeply concerned as indicated by her furrowed forehead. The proportion of annoyance overtook the other two emotions when the Grand Magister cleared his throat and took the liberty of speaking before her. He clapped his hands together as he spoke.

"You're awake! Wonderful," said Harold, he was mostly bald but had wisps of curly, brownish hair. "Simply wonderful. We've all been terribly worried about you. You had hardly made a peep in almost four weeks."

"Miss Candent... how do you... feel?" the High Sage asked.

I told her that I felt rather unwell. The High Sage persisted and asked that I expound upon my answer, and suggested a scale of one to ten. I wasn't quite sure how one ought to translate an oscillating void which felt as if it wrapped around each atom in my body, and was stroking each proton with a claw.

"Can you repeat the question?" I said, sort of looking off into the inviting sunlight through the open window.

The High Sage looked at Harold and then back at me. "I'm going to speak with the other Sages and see if perhaps we can't find another remedy to better serve your needs."

She warped away with the all-too-familiar bzzting that we mages grow up hearing. The Grand Magister stroked his grown-for-upcoming-winter beard and snapped his chubby finger, and a black leather chair materialized under him as he sat in it. He leaned towards me, staring into my eyes intensely. His eyes were a similar light brown to his son's. His gaze evoked a sense of a kindred soul.

"Do you have any recollection of the events preceding your admission to this hospital?" he asked.

I felt a fiery pain and an image of Tobias and frenetic sounds flashed across my mind. I yelped Marvin's name and would have lurched forward had Harold's managrasp not been holding me still. A good thing, too – the movement would have been quite painful.

"No need for all that excitement," he said, his voice deep and soothing. "You need not be frightened, you're currently quite safe."

"Where's Marvin? Is Marvin okay?"

"He's a Hardbub, my dear. He might be among the less-hardy of the Hardbubs... but he's okay," said Harold. "He's in another room."

I asked if I could go over and see Marvin, and he said yes, but then repeated his request. He wished for me to inform him of the nature of the events that led to my residence in that hospital bed. It was sort of hazy, but I could pull back the pieces and roughly stitch them together. The Umbrumes. The Somnumes. *All you have to do, is choose.* More of it came back to me as I searched my mind, and my soul. My manipulating Marvin, the three of us sneaking into the Vault, the arcane books embedded with Blood Magic, and Shadow Magic, and other dark things. I recalled how our attempted thievery resulted in that period of timelessness, that becoming of a forgotten nothingness.

The hairs on the back of my neck raised as I recollected how we were suspended, like rag dolls. We had been dispersed into a void unending, and yet we were also corporeal. It was an unpleasant paradox. The searing reddish light whirled me around and etched dread into each atom in my body. It stroked my soul with its claws as if I were a mouse for it to play with. I told the Grand Magister how I appeared in a dreadful realm, and I told him about the vaguely humanoid beings I saw that had watched and mocked me. I told Harold of the Noc'raakan, and the terrifying realization about the war we're fighting in. For thousands of years, we were struggling against but a fraction of their total power.

"Da'raakan is but my shortest finger," I said, quoting the demonic entities, gasping as I was pulled out of the memory.

I looked at the Grand Magister, whose face had gone pale. He looked deeply alarmed. High Sage Antoinette reappeared and, looking at my face, asked sternly if the Grand Magister had overstayed his welcome. I said that he had not. As a matter of fact, his presence was the only thing grounding me to reality. His presence was a comforting anchor without which I felt I would have been promptly catapulted back into that placeless abyss.

The High Sage pulled out a small bottle from her white raiment, her silky clothes radiated a cloud of blueberry, and she took out the cork. Antoinette tilted the bottle slightly, carefully retrieving a single berry-looking sort of thing the size of a marble. She handed it to me, and I ate it. It was crunchy and profoundly bitter. It was bitter the way only a magic medicine could ever aspire to be. It was the sort of bitterness the very thought of which makes you wince even years after the fact. I scrunched my face in disgust.

"Awful, aren't they?" said Harold. "And they say the Alvish made sweet wines of them. I doubt it, really."

"It is supposed to *heal* her, to alleviate her pain," said the

High Sage. "Forgive me if it fails in possessing the epicurean qualities of which you are so fond, Harold."

The Grand Magister smirked and raised an eyebrow at her which seemed to me to suggest that they had partaken in this dance, and possibly other dances, many times. My thoughts on this were added upon by her almost-suppressed blush.

"In any case, Aylene... there's something... strange... that we need to tell you," she continued. "I'm afraid we've never seen anything like it before."

"Hmm?"

"Well..." began the High Sage, before stopping herself. She looked rather flustered. "The other Sages and I have scoured every medical text we can think of, and we still haven't determined what it could possibly be."

"No one's found a damn thing," said the Grand Magister as he crossed his arms. He looked as if he was deeply contemplating what I had told him.

"Well, what is it?" I asked, growing annoyed with the beat-around-the-bush.

They looked at each other, and back at me, and the High Sage placed her hand on my shoulder.

"It appears..." said Harold, "and when I say *appears* I do mean *appears,* because it is perfectly plausible that the means of detection are somehow eluding... all of us..."

Before Harold finished, he turned to the High Sage, and he nodded his head as a gesture for her to complete his efforts.

"It appears," she said, "that, somehow, you do not have a heartbeat, though it is important to emphasize a possible shortcoming in our abilities to detect it."

My hand shot up and placed two fingers on the veins of my neck. Nothing. Nothing. Da-nothing; I had made the sound in my head but there was no pulse. I did, however, feel that rather peculiar emptiness, the periodic stroking of a void inside my being.

"What's wrong with me?"

"It's almost certainly Shadow Magic, of some sort or other," she said. "It may be that your aura was damaged and needs time to regenerate. You appear to be in perfect health otherwise, save for your soreness."

Oh. I asked if my mother and aunt had been informed of my admission to the hospital. They had not, in accordance with my preferences as indicated on my medical authorizations at the Academy. How was I going to tell them? What would I even tell them? I asked if I would be able to return to school in the Spring semester. The High Sage told me she would be speaking with the Academy's Arch Mage, and would give him updates on my health.

"By the way, Aylene," asked Antoinette. "As much as I do not wish to press you, do you remember anything? Anything at all?"

Harold shook his head ever-so-slightly. His face was so grim and serious, and I said that I did not. Why didn't he want me to tell her? The High Sage turned to Harold and they whispered in magically-encrypted words. They were veiling their intentions such that it would have been impossible for anyone but an expert in Magicryptography to decipher their meaning. They stopped talking after a few minutes and turned to face me again. Seeing as I just awoke, the High Sage told me they needed to continue to monitor my condition.

If nothing changed, I would be released in a week under the care of two Crystal Constructs... "Until such a time that we are satisfied with the long-term stability of your health."

Harold's eyes twinkled with a mischievous delight, and he twirled his fingers in an upward arc through the air and told me, "You'll be out of here in time for Yesteryear!"

"High Sage," I asked, speaking quietly. "Would it be alright if I spoke to the Grand Magister in private?"

She raised her eyebrows at me. This clearly alarmed her suspicions. I said that it was about Herbert, and she nodded and warped out of the room. The two Crystal Constructs in the room, which would follow me in later times, stood in position towards the back of the room. I gestured towards them, not even saying words, but the two of them beeped firmly in perfect unison. 'I see.'

"Do not let them disturb your sense of privacy," said Harold. "Their programming includes patient confidentiality. They understand, and, for the most part, shall listen to your intentions."

"What's going to happen to Tobias?" I asked, although I already knew what Harold's pronouncement would likely be.

"If what you've said is true, and I have no reason to believe otherwise," said the Grand Magister, "if Tobias is apprehended, he will face trial, and shall be charged as an oathbreaker."

I looked into his eyes and mentioned that, as far as we knew at the time, we were forced into action. Harold reminded me that the laws regarding the usage of Dark Magic are, for better or for worse, relatively inflexible. I responded quickly and said it wasn't Tobias; he wasn't the caster. Without flinching, the Grand Magister quoted the ruling established in Erezoth v. the High Council, 1688. *"In accordance with Justice, the law shall not distinguish between the creator(s) and intentional activator(s), if they differ, of incantations or any other manifestations of spirit that violate the Laws of Light. In all such cases, each of the accused bears full and equal responsibility and shall be sentenced to death.*" I asked why it was, then, that I would not be charged, expelled, and sentenced to death. My actions had, I felt, directly contributed to Dark Magic harming an individual outside of the context of self-defence. I deceived Marvin, so was I not equally to blame?

"Had you any awareness that your deception, and the taking of this Umbrume," said Harold, "would in any way involve the Dark Magic which resulted in your hospitalization?"

I shook my head, tearing up.

"When compelled by an actor of darkness to make a choice," he continued, "did you act honourably? Did you by any words or other means indicate your willingness to cause harm to befall Marvin? Was it you who attempted to sacrifice my nephew?"

Hot tears streamed down my cheeks, and I felt awful. I tried wiping them away, but it was fruitless. The Grand Magister pressed me further, staring into my soul with an intensity not so different from the Faceless. But Harold's judgement came from a soul of light and Honora. I shook my head and told him no. And so the head of my nation pronounced to me my innocence, stating that, despite my role in initiating the events, my actions were free from malice and intent. Unless my statements were contradicted by future testimony or extracted information, I was innocent. I would not receive the charges as faced by Tobias.

"If I am innocent," I asked – my voice sounded pathetic – "*why do I feel so ashamed?*"

"Because you were manipulative, there's no question about that. And what has happened to you and Marvin is terrible. My nephew's condition is characterized by the sporadic vomiting of blood, and frequent nightmares, and the occasional seizure. I am of course disappointed in you; but I will not judge you so harshly all the same. You acted not with malice, but misguided curiosity, perhaps indulging a familial feline weakness, if your Lion crest is anything to go by," said Harold with a slight bow of his head and a world-weary smile.

Harold stood up, dissipated the chair, and spoke to me one last time before he warped away. "With the luck of the Mother's dice, may you always remember that not all knowledge is worth knowing. I shall take my leave, and may you have a full and swift recovery."

Chapter 14

Reading Light

In defiance of the beeps and chirps of protest emitted by the Crystal Constructs assigned to me, I rose from my hospital bed and left the room. A pleasant smile and an air of nonchalance ensured that the random Sages I happened upon didn't stop me with questions. It's a wonderful trick to know, really – remember it well. If you look busy, and walk with purpose, you will likely not be stopped. The Constructs lumbered behind me to the beat of my stubborn stride as I searched the hospital. It has been said that I am, for better or for worse, intrinsically opposed to asking for assistance. I am inclined to disagree and posit that my hierarchy of values simply places a greater weighting on independence. In any case, I was determined to find Marvin, if but through the unrelenting force of my will, in defiance of significant discomfort. It was because of me that Marvin had been in the hospital for around a month; it was because of me he had been having seizures.

If my experience was anything to go by, I would say that you're quite likely to see some rather unpleasant things while walking around a magi hospital. In particular, I remember a strikingly-old white-haired moustached fellow, sitting on his bed and reading a newspaper. The flesh on both of his legs was defiled by gnarled spikes of bone which jutted through his skin like deformed rib cages. He was arguing with a Sage, his eyes never leaving the newspaper, about his fundamental rights as a wounded veteran to partake of his pipe. A pipe which, I could see, she had confiscated.

"Lung cancer?" he scoffed, his face red and indignant as he lowered his newspaper. "Look at my legs! My eyesight has seen better years of youth, I'll grant you that, but even I can detect that there are *bones* protruding from my stumps. Imagine that. I didn't serve my country for fifty-seven years to be told not to smoke my Goddamn pipe."

The Constructs turned towards me and beeped in near unison. Indeed, he did seem rather feisty. The veteran in question looked towards my direction and noticed me watching him. His face was red with exasperation. He must have been curious as to why exactly I had Constructs assigned to me. Before he had time to call out and ask, or mention anything to the Sage beside him, I hurried away. I tried and failed to ignore the other various sufferings I saw, the Dark Magic scars which quite possibly would never fully heal. A missing eye, a woman whose ears were leaking blood. Sages here, Sages there, all of them with their determined faces, with their clipboards, pens and their arsenal of eclectic magical apparatuses. The ball-point pen, in case you are wondering, is one of the many inventions of the laypeople that magi rely on in our daily lives. And yes, we use cell phones... who wouldn't?"

"Marvin?" I asked, my voice hesitant, when I found his room and walked in slowly.

"Aylene! You're finally awake. Oh my goodness..." said Marvin. "We're going to play so much Glyphwalkers, Herbert tried to go see y- huh?"

I scurried closer to his bed and smiled as I gestured towards the Constructs, "Oh, don't worry, they're harmless."

Marvin sat up and pushed his glasses back above his nose. Now closer to him, I noticed a strong resemblance in facial structure between him, Herbert, and the Grand Magister. They all had boyish faces and kind brown eyes. Marvin was just more petite, Herbert taller and in better, firmer shape, and Harold much wider.

"I'm actually quite familiar with Automatons," said Marvin, squinting at me from behind his glasses. "I know how to program them. Say, umm... did any of the Sages mention anything to you about the letters... floating above your head?"

"The what?"

Marvin leaned towards me, his eyes squinting through the blue frames, and gestured strange motions as if he was playing with a Rubik's cube. He sat back and told me that he had determined the letters were Alvish, and that they were very hard to see. Some kind of obscuring magic had rendered the words almost undetectable. Furthermore, the fact that only he seemed to be able to observe them indicated that they were in some way connected to the Umbrume's backlash.

"Oh... I wanted to talk to you about that..." I said, my voice softened with shame. "Do you remember anything about what happened?"

Marvin sat back and tried to recall the events, shook his head, and then started vomiting blood. I basically had a panic attack. A Sage scurried in and used a sensing spell to scan him. Her hand glowed as energy wrapped around it like a cloud of white and orange. The mess of curse-defiled blood sparkled into dust and evaporated while Marvin tried to calm down and stop gasping and heaving. He thanked her, and he explained to me that it was just an aftershock. As surely as the Raconds are regarded

116

for their fiery temper are the Hardbub's known as an enduring sort of people ("hardy as a Hardbub" is a commonly used colloquialism). The Sage left and said she would be around momentarily if anything else happened.

"Marvin, I'm so sorry." My voice was shaking, and I was crying. It seemed that happened a lot. "I should never have tricked you."

He shrugged, readjusted his glasses, and told me that we were lucky to be alive. Marvin reminded me that unintentionally-activated Umbrumes have resulted in things a great deal worse. There is a lengthy list of backlashes which includes a variety of deaths; some of the least unpleasant were electrocution and boiling blood.

"You wanted to see more things," he said, smiling. "I understand... I was the one who showed you Somnumes. They're incredible, and they're one of the main reasons I find the Darmer fascinating. It's okay, Aylene, I forgive you. I know you didn't mean to get us hurt. You owe me a lot of Glyphwalkers, though."

I thanked my friend and squeezed his hand in my hands, and then right before I let go, he said, "Wait! Don't move!"

Marvin was gripping my wrist. It felt as if a small current of electricity was going through me.

He had a face of disbelief. "I can read the words... that's... that's incredible!"

He let go of my wrist, put his hand on my arm again, and his eyes widened as he informed me that our contact temporarily gave him 'understanding'. Marvin described it as being like reading, except the words still look completely foreign, but the meaning comes anyway. It sounded to me like when the Faceless void chose to blast words into my being, but less unpleasant. To read Alvish, I have heard since childhood, is to hear the distant musicality of the Higher Heavens, to hear the whispered words which chime like bells. Alvish. A language which, until this happened, our scholars had only managed to decipher just a couple hundred words of.

"We need to speak to the Grand Magister."

Chapter 15

The City of Gold

The healers figured out what incantation was tormenting Marvin. It ended up being Blood Magic. They found a reference to it in an arcane tome. A carefully traced counter spell negated the incantation and dispelled it. I was in the room when the counter spell was performed by a Sage named Colette, a little brown-haired healer from France. She had the robes of white and gold that so many healers wore. Her hands were tattooed in silver ink with the geometric matrix known as the 'Seal of Seraphim', the bodily signature of the Oath of Benevolence. They glowed a whitish-orange as she dispelled Marvin. The procedure took less than a minute and the Hardbub was as good as new, and quite chipper. Chipper enough for his justified insistence of a few matches of Glyphwalkers. Repeated and emphatic instruction had previously ensured Herbert's actually bringing the cards in question, which he kept forgetting to do. It is difficult perhaps to politely and thoughtfully decline a request to a game when asked by a sickly cousin in a hospital.

Marvin was released from the hospital, but I was still under observation for three more days at the time of his departure. The Behemoth Constructs stayed in my room and periodically beeped and chirped to see if there was anything I needed. It was pretty boring. I occasionally, but only very briefly, perused some of the volumes on the bookshelves in the corner of my room. I spoke to my mother and aunt a couple of times, although I acted as though I were still at school. I also talked to Herbert, though my conversations with him were rather briefer than I would've liked. We hadn't spoken about it directly, yet, but by his distance, I suspected that he knew enough about what happened to be quite upset with me.

On the day I was discharged, the High Sage woke me up. We reviewed paperwork and medical terminology, and she obtained my signature. My condition was no longer causing distress, nor had it revealed any additional symptoms. It did not match the diagnostic criteria of any spell on record, so they decided I was ready to be released. If, of course, being released was in accordance with my wishes (it was; I get terrible cabin fever). It was also dependent on the final approval of the Grand Magister. Furthermore, to my surprise, it would ultimately be Harold who would be escorting me back to campus after some business in Lunaris. He was going to take me to our sky-held capital, the city of my birth, a city I had not been in for nearly ten years.

Above the earth, beneath the clouds, is a city invisible to all except its current occupants. It is undetectable by radar and satellite, and it is obscured by ancient magic. No technology the laypeople currently or would ever possess could hope to detect it. Lunaris is veiled by magic so that no plane could ever possibly collide with our blessed city. The city is accessible only via warp stones which are so heavily guarded that not even Da'raakan and his myriad of Demons and Dark Mages could breech the 'gates'. Even the codes, the exact and lengthy combination of magic runes and glyphs… even the 'password' changed daily.

The City of Gold, with her unparalleled beauty, our city in the sky which my ancestors reclaimed by force. In Lunaris, at sunset, you see not one sun, but two orange blossom twins. Two stars, or else one and its reflection, colliding into oneness. The golden rays were so bright I squinted until my eyes adjusted. All around us in every direction were the crystal towers wherein so many of our people lived.

We magi call this city home. They lived inside rooms of the buildings, the angularity of which make them look like cut gems. I teared up a bit as I stood there, looking up at the regal skyline, the city where my heart belonged since childhood. This was the city my mother and aunt had been banished from, the city my father had been executed in. And now I returned, not redeemed, but ashamed.

The Twin Stars were quite content with their incessant shining. The two distinct flows of warmth are interwoven into such perfect harmony so as to be indistinguishable for the untrained mind. Harold produced a handkerchief from one of the many pockets in his suit raiment. His clothes were black, formal, but not excessively so, stylish and expensive and tasteful. How odd it was, that we were here together.

"What makes one hungrier than a distant warp, hmm?" asked Harold. "Other than being a Hardbub, of course! Might I suggest we find something to eat?"

I smiled back at him weakly and nodded, shifting my weight from foot to foot. I breathed in, I held my breath. I wanted to start walking, and right as I finally did so, I exhaled as if I had not breathed in years. I still had no heartbeat as I followed him out of the warp plaza, but I felt life in me anyways. I saw the flowers of every shade and degree of opaqueness, from friendly pastel petals to leaves of audacious vibrancy. The air wafted with

121

aromatic fruits, the scent of which was rich despite the distance. Here and there the bushes held translucent flowers, the petals of which looked as if they were made of glass as thin as paper. The Crystal Constructs lumbered behind us clumsily, and each 'footstep' of the massive slabs boomed as they walked. My made-of-stone chaperones. What a sight we must have been.

The daughter of a banished household, and the Grand Magister himself - and he was sober, which he rarely was. The children were whooshing through their magic streets, girls chasing boys and boys chasing girls, innocent and joyous. Some of their parents were sitting on the glass benches and smiling as the little ones played. There was a tangible merriment, as if just being there was like being charged with electric happiness. Harold wished to satiate his hunger as quickly as possible, but I begged him to let me look around some of the shops, which I had not seen since I was a little girl.

What strange, fantastic places. Through the windows of *Mr. Beasties*, I saw the creatures that the more affluent of magi children (and the others who received them as gifts) kept as pets. Pyrinines are roughly the size of and vaguely resemble a Maine Coon cat, but are technically a chimera based more closely on the genetics of dogs. Where an ordinary creature had fur, they had lukewarm flames, and they loved being cuddled. They were little scamps; mischievous, intelligent and affectionate. Their milk is used in our magic hot cocoa equivalent, Choconut Sunrises.

Rather less intelligent, comically so, were the Balloon Lizards. They are like bearded dragons. Affectionate, but they're as goofy as if they had been bred for clumsiness. Their backs are covered with small gem-like scales of ostentatious colours, and underneath their armpits they have fleshy pink sacs which they can almost instantly inflate. They suck in a huge gulp of air, and, baffling even the most advanced Transmutationists, fill their sacs with what is temporarily helium. This lets them float, and they seem rather content to float about, exhaling and inhaling as necessary to inflate or deflate, to ascend and descend. They use this to push themselves away from colliding with walls and towards each other. Curiously, especially in the presence of groups of children, the creatures actually seem to intentionally collide. Funny little things.

Invisiphants are pygmy elephants the size of a large dog, and they can change their colour to cloak themselves. They're quite happy to hide and toot their trunks to give you hints as to where they've chosen to conceal themselves. Give one a handful of peanuts and you'll have made a best friend. An Invisiphant never forgets; not if you offer it peanuts. Viofinches are birds, the feathers of which come in a gradient of melancholic purples, and their songs vaguely resemble a violin. Their songs are always overwhelmingly joyous, or exceptionally depressing.

Wartles are turtles with long, thick and oddly-shaped tusks, as if the original maker of the species was an entomologist with a fascination with stag beetles. The Wartles take great pleasure in a sort of wrestling game wherein the females attempt to flip each other. The males observe this and bob their heads up and down in anticipation of union with the victor. That's just to name a handful. There's a bunch of other beasties and critters, if you have the Scriggets to pay for one.

Oh! That's right, Scriggets. Simply put, a Scrigget is the currency used by American magi primarily for non-laypeople goods. Scriggets are unique in that they are impossible to replicate, far more colourful (thank goodness), and the pictures thereon shift throughout the months of the year. They're very festive and it's an absolute nightmare to produce a counterfeit. A funny titbit of magi culture is that it is actually *illegal* to sell a bottled pop for more, or less, than one Scrigget (The Principals of Magic Economics, Chapter Four, Misadventures in Inflation). At least you know what a Scrigget's worth: a tasty, magically-brewed soda, with a metal cap, and a seal of authenticity.

While I played with a few critters, Harold drank a Howdy Neighbour. They're made with the fermented fruit of a cactus alongside a couple of other magic ingredients which, apparently, "fill you with the courage of the Wild West". I'm more of a Monkey's Uncle girl myself, that soda puts you in a light-hearted mood. Those are made with peanut butter and chocolate and are fizzy and creamy like an ice cream float. I left the store after a few minutes, and I re-joined Harold and the Constructs. The three of them were standing outside the store and looked rather conspicuous. Children were pointing at the pair of Constructs, and their curious inquiries were responded to with controlled but upbeat chirps.

The Grand Magister, in accordance with our holiday customs and festivities, is regarded by children with a reverence that closely resembles Santa Claus. Harold's roundness of tum, the ferocity of his winter-worn and magically-whitened beard... his *proclivity* for sweetened boons, often filled with Stormeye Rum; he jokes he was born to play the part. The Grand Magister was quite fond of being an inebriated similar-to-Santa.

The Grand Magister asked me if I wanted a pop and I smiled and nodded eagerly. He handed the moustached man running the pop cart one Scrigget and a generous tip, and I retrieved a Monkey's Uncle with a grin that'd rival even the Hardbubs. We continued our casual stroll. Harold stopped periodically to point at a few of the stores of particular noteworthiness, asking me if I remembered them. There was *The Meticulous Mage,* where the more dignified mages went to have their hair cut. Their chief rival was the *Boxed Barber* across the street from them. Their building was intentionally enchanted so as to resemble a ramshackle thrown-together building of questionable structural integrity. They advertise their price as being *"The Meticulous Mage minus one Scrigget!"* which was, understandably, profoundly annoying to the owners of the other salon. Harold preferred the *Boxed Barber*, naturally, and not simply because they served complementary alcohol to the patrons on the weekends. He also occasionally fought on 'Fisticuffs Friday'.

The *Elixir Emporium* sold various potions, wines, spirits and liquors with a remarkably wide assortment of secondary effects. The *Wuffpuffery* sold incense, tobacco, spices, herbs, pipes and hookahs. The city had a myriad of restaurants of many ethnic varieties of food, some magi related, and some essentially laypeople cuisine. We even have a Chipotle! The Grand Magister had a couple of corporate-minded folk in upper management that made that happen without alerting suspicion. A music store, a video game store, a dollar store (*Just A Scrigget),* and so many others. The last I'll name is the one that I am perhaps the fondest of: *Of Clouds,* clothing described as being as soft as clouds. Battle raiment, formal attire, sundresses, their fanciest clothing transcends such boundaries.

The price cards below the adorned figurines said only the word *"Inquire"* in fanciful script. It's often said that if you're afraid to ask, it costs too much. Whoever first said that was probably right. My heartbeat would have skipped a beat, had it a beat to skip, and I stared through the glass windows for a half minute with my jaw dropped. I had never been very fond of dresses, but every now and again life shows you something that challenges your presupposed preferences. I turned and walked

125

away.

"Aylene!" barked the Grand Magister. "I'm afraid I must inquire as to where exactly you think you're going."

I turned around and blushed. "Why tempt myself? I can't afford anything they're selling. And I don't deserve a dress like that, anyway."

"I see," said Harold, stroking his beard. "Though, perhaps, is it not worth considering that the grandeur of the upcoming festive occasion necessitates the wearing of a lovely thing, as such?"

To his credit, the magi equivalent to a combined Christmas and New Year's Eve, Yesteryear, was on the horizon. Our people celebrate the day, and evening, with extremely rowdy exuberance.

I rolled my eyes at the Grand Magister, with his formal speech, the subtleties of which the Highborn are taught in childhood, our eloquence enhanced by magic. "Unless I'm to finance the acquisition of such a thing by thievery, sir, then I am without recourse. By all accounts, I appear to have already exceeded my acquisition attempts for enchanted-or-cursed possessions."

"My son's heart included. What if, perhaps," he said, his brown eyes twinkling, "the Hardbub household was able to assist you with such an acquisition? You two shall dance, I imagine, clumsy oaf that he is if he takes after his father, which in most ways he doesn't."

I shook my head. "As generous as that offer is, Grand Magister... err... Mister Hardbub? As appreciative as I am, I cannot accept it. My mother and aunt can't afford such luxuries and it would be in poor taste for me to possess such a lavish thing."

The Hardbubs are a proud and generous sort of people. The Grand Magister scoffed and gestured for me to take a look around. I didn't know why he was being so nice to me... I certainly didn't think I deserved it. We were at an impasse, it seemed, and he would not budge... fine. I shifted my weight from foot to foot, nervous and uncomfortable. Maybe I could sell it another day and give the money to my mom. She needed it. It wasn't her fault, none of it was, and I felt horrible for what she had been through.

The two of us walked into the store and he told the woman, Miss Shavam, that he would be billing the expense to the Hardbub family account. I think she and I both had a look of disbelief, and for her, seeing my face was probably as surprising as seeing the Grand Magister. The crystalline stone boulder things seemed quite content to stand outside the store entrance. The shopkeeper asked me if I needed help finding anything. I declined. I had seen the article which most captivated me the instant I looked through the window. It was a light sky blue with dreamy clouds drifting across the cloth, a magic perpetually-moving pattern. They even recharge passively through the mana emitted from your aura.

I walked closer to it and examined a small card. After touching it, the word 'inquire' changed to a paragraph which informed me that the dress was enchanted so as to be: height-adjusting, unwrinkleable, self-healing, self-cleaning, gender-malleable, borrow auto-returning, impervious to liquid, resistant to magic, mood-matching and formality-assessing. And best of all, it generated pockets as needed, or when desired.

I gulped nervously, a little afraid as to what I was getting the Grand Magister into. I knew the Hardbubs were affluent but... I don't know. It's an uncomfortable thing, not having money, having so little and being given something so valuable, so casually. As if it was nothing to him; as if it was little more than the soda he'd gotten for me earlier. The dress was about to become my loveliest possession, except for the few pieces of jewellery my mother kept for me, following the reparations. Uncomfortable. Guilt. Extravagance, unnecessary, materialistic. Wasted on me. I had touched the dress and found it as soft as the clouds by which the store was figuratively named. I wanted to get out and run away, Constructs be damned.

Miss Shavam walked over and clapped her hands together enthusiastically, apparently pleased with either my choice in fashion, or else the exorbitant cost of the selected item. Perhaps both? Probably. She smiled at me, told me that I had lovely taste, and that the dress was amongst her favourites. She put her hand on my back and walked me to the front of the store where Harold was standing, now donning full-moon sunglasses with arms crossed and his white, bearded grin.

Miss Shavam pulled a box from beneath the counter and turned around and opened a drawer, pulling out one of those dresses. She folded it perfectly, and placed it in a lovely pink bag made of Sky Silk. I thanked Harold at least ten times. I could feel the warmth of blood rushing to my face. My cheeks were a scarlet quite brighter than my hair. I told him that, from that day, until the end of my days, I would treasure that box and that dress. They would forever remind me of my return to the City of Gold, and my few hours with the Grand Magister. It was that lovely day before which my life would again change forever, when Harold Hardbub ordered my relocation to a military research station. My undiagnosed, not-quite-an-affliction was declared a government secret, "Level Echo".

Chapter 16

Level Echo

At a classified location, accessed by a specific hidden Warpstone, with an entry code which changes regularly, is the United Magisterium's military research centre. The creative efforts of our architects, although admirable, do little to lessen the oppressive feeling of being confined to the colourlessness of that facility. The furniture conformed not to aesthetic ideals, but to pragmatic functionality. The bedrooms were essentially closets with a cot, a dresser, and a table stand. The walls are entirely uniform, a grey metal with dulled hints of brown, a formulation that is almost completely impervious to magic. A metal, the properties of which are such that a nuclear explosion would not leave a single scratch, invented by the Darmer.

There were no windows. The complex was illuminated by a harsh yellowish light which was so intense that it affected my sleep. Even once I left the common plaza to sleep in my room, the overwhelming brightness left me dizzy. Had I known that the acquisition of my enchanted dress would precede my compulsory relocation to this military station... perhaps I would have reconsidered. I say this in jest; in reality the reasons underlying my formally-ordered relocation were in accordance with the interests of our national, and global, security. Another unfortunate aspect of my circumstances was the loss of usage of my phone, and the internet. Electricity was suppressed.

All inbound and outbound communication, the Grand Magister included, was conducted via a network of Acosignos, magically-encrypted devices which could transmit, record and output sound. My first day at the research centre involved a tour escorted by one of the few people with whom I would have consistent contact: Margarette Hardbub, the Grand Magister's older sister, and Marvin's mom. She kept her greying hair in a tightly-wrapped bun and always wore these large circular glasses with mirror-like lenses; you only see your reflection in them. Her style of dress was perfunctory to say the least: grey and black raiment which protected her neck, and matching gloves. Like my newly acquired dress, her clothes were magic resistant.

My tour began with the Arcanium. A particularly massive library filled with several thousand codexes, Somnumes, Umbrumes, and glyph books. Many of the books had developed personalities, and some of the Spirits were over two thousand years old. Some were discovered in Lunaris and other ancient cities, Hastinapur and Alexandria in particular. Inside this labyrinth, there were a handful of tomes which were so powerful they required 'Darmathenes' to contain them. A Darmathene is a twisted cage of criss-crossing metal which wraps around and squeezes a glass sphere. I looked at the ancient machine in front of me. The interlocked gears rotated and clicked together with barely-perceivable hums and insect chitters. There was the occasional burst of screeching steam-esque mana vapor as a by-product of the machines' movements.

At the centre of these Darmish machines were glass spheres inscribed with constantly moving and shifting runes. At the very centre of the sphere was a single book. Those are the books that we are supposed to leave alone, under all conditions. The machines that protect them have somewhere between twenty and thirty magical ways to kill you simultaneously. The parallel explosions and bursts of different-coloured flames are accompanied by blinding light. There is a surge of lightning-strength electricity, followed by boiling blood and other arcane unpleasantries. Survival is essentially impossible. Good luck trying to provide a precise answer so as to negate the exact combinations of magic which disintegrated your body.

Two of these Darmathenes, as I would learn, were the vessels containing parts of the essences of two of the Noc'raakan, also known as 'Ascended Titans'. They are the primordial manifestations of destruction which the Alvish worked rather diligently to contain. They are embodied void, with near-deity power levels. They are the nightmares of our childhood, and adulthood. Even looking towards one of their Darmathenes strained your body. It was as if it was adding weight to your shoulders, and, once you gave in, you would be snatched from your existence and enter their abode.

"That is quite troubling," said Margarette after I finished explaining my experience.

The energy the Darmathenes gave off was nearly identical. The entities were different fingers, on the same hand.

There was an awkward silence until the Grand Magister spoke. "Until recently we were under the impression that there were only three, two of which are successfully, if partially, encapsulated in machines in this room. How generous the Alvish were to entrust us with their family heirlooms. We assumed that Da'raakan... was the only one remaining."

Harold continued. "A more pessimistic fellow than myself, Miss Candent, would be rather distraught at your having quite possibly awakening an entity that, quite possibly, would not have bothered us for a couple of millennia. It is certainly inconvenient; I would have much preferred this occurrence to have occurred during the leadership of the successor to my successor's successor, and so on times a hundred. I am not particularly keen, to tell you the truth, of it being under an era of Hardbub that every living being on this planet experiences the fate of cataclysmic annihilation."

The unpleasant feeling of having my soul scraped with nails of darkness became more pronounced as Harold spoke. It was like there was a bubble of shadow inside of me that heard the words and was titillated by such destructive prospects.

"But I have hope in me yet, Miss Candent," said Harold, wagging a rather heavy finger at me in existential panic. "That curiosity of yours has felicitously been accompanied by a new resource that, I daresay… perhaps my optimism is delusional, ah - well… it is quite possible that you have, by accident, become the key we have been searching for."

Margarette put her hand on my shoulder and squeezed me in a manner which, if attempting to comfort me, did a poor job at accomplishing that task. I quickly felt nauseous. I felt cold perspiration forming beads on my neck and back, and my skin felt aflame with agitation. It is with great difficulty that one resists the void. It is like gravity; you can jump up to defy it, momentarily. But just as surely it will humble your efforts as it pulls you to the ground. I could not jump; but I could stand in defiance of my burden.

"Would you pull the Umbrume for me, Harold?" she asked as she shuffled through her notes.

Harold levitated the book with a managrasp with a casual flick of the wrist. He kept it in the air there, floating. Margarette called me over, and instructed me to touch the book; they had already determined that this book had no curses. The moment the pages opened I felt a sort of magnetic pulse from the book. I saw light, I heard light, and I felt light. For a short moment, I once again heard the choral music of Alvish singing. The light gave way to the pain of those increasingly-familiar nails scraping my metaphysical being. The sensation morphed into voidfire. As I collapsed towards the floor, Harold negated the force. He lifted me up, and conjured a rather comfortable chair, which he then sat me upon. I felt like a bell had smashed into me and then the reverberations were pulsing through me like I was jelly. I felt an abrupt flash of sorrow as I was reminded of what Marvin had been subjected to.

"Harold."

The two of them talking sounded so distant; I could have easily not been there at all. I wasn't there, I was somewhere else. Tired. What a trying thing existence is. How much it asked of me.

"Harold, it… it appears to have worked. It has been deciphered."

"Is it gibberish?"

I heard the flipping of wrinkled pages. "It is not."

"Are you sure?" he asked. His voice was incredulous.

"I am."

"Well, I'll be damned. The only problem is this seems to be rather trying on our young friend here. Aylene?"

"Miss Candent? Unresponsive… hmm. We *cannot* by any means allow her to leave this facility," said Margarette. "They would find her within months, maybe weeks. She is the key we have been searching for."

"It's going to be like looking for a needle in a haystack," said Harold, apprehensive. "That was just one book. We will proceed only with her consent, and only so long as we are making steady

133

progress to improve upon the process. Let us hope, then, that we do. Pass the message along to Von Bear."

Demonic gravity withstood, I rose, and pushed myself off the chair. I stood to face the two government officials whose actions directly shaped the lives of every living being on our planet. The head of our nation, the equivalent of a president, the Grand Magister. And his sister, one of the keenest minds, one of our top scientists. Her diligent research efforts were backed by optimism; she believed we would find a way to maintain the barrier that protected our plane of existence. It is one thing to deal with rifts, or the leaked bubble of a small Demon. It is another thing altogether to prevent a wave of death from enveloping the universe. The boundary that protected us was eroding. It was being gnawed, slashed, crushed, and burnt away in every moment, as Da'raakan's servants worked unceasingly.

And so I resigned myself to serving as an embodied translation, a blessing and a curse in equal parts. "I have a need to redeem myself, and I will give my life if ever it need be."

Chapter 17

Books Within Books

It began as a day that seemed to be like any other, with a quick brief before an expedition. We had been analysing books within books within books. The other two confluence members were on their way, and I was in the room with Walking Blizzard and the Grand Magister. Margarette was looking through some of her notes in the other room. Walking Blizzard (Madison's mother), was the Confluence commander, and I assure you she leaves an impression upon all whom she encounters. Her skin is dark, and her eyes are a piercing arctic blue filled with swirling snowflakes. Her aura radiates frost, and liquid water that goes near her freezes. She usually eats by magically absorbing frozen food. Even when she *spoke* to you, you felt cold. Whether or not this elemental characteristic contributed significantly to her less-than-talkative nature is a mystery unsolved.

An impartial onlooker might regard my sentiments as sophomoric. But I did in truth resonate with vague notions of what a whaler of times past might have felt before going on an oceanic, bloody excursion. Herbert and his warmth, and his cooking, were niceties that I would deeply miss. In evaluating the appropriateness (or excessiveness) of my enraptured affection for my Hardbub, I will add a dash of context that I have not already mentioned. Because of our nobility, and the geometries of our birth charts, Herbert and I were originally betrothed shortly after my birth. A fated union, the arrangement of which dissipated instantaneously upon the actions of my father. My father, who, in one day, upended hundreds of years of the Lion's legacy.

I was myself hard of heart (and would grow more steely still), save for my Hardbubs, and my aunt, and my mother. They were the other Candents upon whom my patriarch's choices had left an irrevocable mark.

It is about they whom one most highly treasures whom thoughts tend towards, in times shortly before, and for a long time after, great peril.

In our dialect of Ameragi English, a cohesive unit of Battlemages is referred to as a 'Confluence'. This word is not absolute; it is a form of plurality that is quite often rhetorically charged. To be a Confluence, a group of individual magi must act in unison. In a Confluence, the incantations and bodily movements and even thoughts flow together like enmeshed waves of water. To be a Confluence is to be a dynamically-expressed melody of separate parts that responds to, and overcomes, obstacles. For soldiers in training, even for the elite students at the prestigious Academy, the term is most frequently sarcastic.

Our not-quite-a-Confluence of three was accidentally assembled.

Margarette, one of our foremost experts in Magilinguistics, and Alvish and Darmish culture and technology, had been analysing our decoded Somnumes and Umbrumes. She had been continually building upon a map through the network. Part of the advances were guided by my magnetic tugs. Others were predicted with mathematical models that used data from tools for Interdimensional Analytics. If we had any chance of capturing the rest of the Noc'raakan in Darmathenes, we needed to develop an understanding of the ancient technologies. Through contact with me, we were able to decrypt Somnumes and Umbrumes without entering them. But the Somnumes were just captured dreams, they were pleasant memories. The Umbrumes contained nestled books within books within books, and often required a quasi-physical exploration.

Our entering of the Umbrume, that day in early December... was an accident.

By tradition, the Grand Magister has to eat the inebriating candies provided by any magi who happen upon him. Harold was wobbling, complaining about a few upcoming meetings, and said he found the details of our expeditions a good deal more interesting. His complaints progressed to ranting. W.B turned around and ignored him as she looked through Confluence profiles. I had long since zoned out.

With a particularly forceful gesture, Harold stumbled backwards and fell towards a desk. I lunged forward to try to stop his fall, without using magic, but I couldn't bear his weight as we crashed onto the desk. His hand landed on the book that his sister had specifically warned the three of us to not touch.

It was a churning turquoise and dark green; it was beautiful in a sinister way. It was an oceanic paradise with subtle hints of the abyss below. The book backlashed, and for half of a second, once again I heard the choral music. The three of us were energized into dots of light. We were catapulted out of our earthly existence, and we entered the encapsulated realm of the Umbrume. W.B's dots poofed into flurries of snow before her final dissipation. Harold's dots bubbled with the hiccup of drunkenness. Mine were two orbiting energies. A mixture of red and shadow energy chased, and was chased by, golden fire. It remained to be seen which of the two duelling forces within my soul would prevail.

Chapter 18

Mayhem in Lunaris

It was a surprisingly pleasant day for early December, the sort of day whereon the winds chastise you only if you stumble about sans sweater. I remember that afternoon quite well; there was an appreciable richness to the sky's unperturbed blue. The professors, acting under the leadership of the Arch Mage, instructed all students to gather at the auditorium, informing them of an emergency broadcast. The projector turned on and all at the Academy - professors, students, and happenstance visitors - found themselves looking forward. The speaker was the Magisterium Press Secretary, Martha Mavella. She was delivering a message live from our glass-building capital.

"Good afternoon. I am delivering this message as authorized and instructed by the Wing Council. At approximately eleven thirty earlier this morning, Grand Magister Hardbub, Walking Blizzard of the Arcane Guard, and Aylene Candent, a first-year student of the Academy, went missing. Arcane Guard Confluences have already been dispatched and several hundred soldiers are conducting a search and rescue operation in this ongoing investigation. The Wing Council has declared an emergency-status level three, meaning all travel into and out of Lunaris has been suspended.

The duration of this travel freeze is currently unclear, and all citizens for whom this causes immediate logistical challenges, including but not limited to shelter, food and water, and medicine, are to contact Citizen Services, 1-800 MAGIGOV. The government is actively working to arrange provisions and accommodations for all such citizens, and has informed us that this may involve occupation at layperson lodgings. Estimates on the number of families that will be disrupted have ranged from twelve hundred to nearly two thousand, and all citizens are asked to remain calm and patient. All families with children under the age of thirteen will receive priority magi housing. All citizens thirteen and older are officially instructed to review Article Four on Layperson Interactions and Affairs.

As of this broadcast, the Wing Council has temporarily assumed command of the Arcane Guard. Finally, it has been asked that you remain vigilant and report any suspicious behaviour. Thank you for your time, and may the Higher Lights guide us."

Chapter 19

Hydroxis

The pleasant froth of wave and bubbles broke against my legs as the water rolled over me. Seagulls squawking in the distance periodically interrupted the peace of the warmth of the sand. The clouds that graced the distant horizon were white, swollen giants. The Himalayan height of the cloud peaks was of such a scale that its contrast with the lower-lying masses of vapor was enthralling. The difference effectively conveyed the magnitude of the sky, and left me feeling rather small, and I jolted up as if a crab had pinched me. One hadn't, but it was a micro-slice of dread, a sort of momentary cosmic fizzling of unpleasantness. More a crab pinch than a mosquito bite; perspective is always important when discussing such topics.

I called out for the Grand Magister, but the only reply was sounds of the tropical forest, and the shore-kissing ocean.

There was a persistent chrrrrrr of wind which whooshed around my red hair as I looked around. "Walking Blizzard!"

I warped around the jungle island, scanning my environment for any signs of Harold or W.B. It was a much larger island than I anticipated, and the constant warping was draining my mana way too quickly. After thirty or forty warps, my rest in-between them increased from seconds to a minute to several minutes. I was not fond of the fact that it seemed those God-like clouds were getting closer. They were coming straight towards us, and something about the shape of the clouds was making me anxious. I had to stop warping. I was out of breath… I heard a stern lesson in the back of my mind as I recalled one of my lectures from the Academy.

"What mistake is the number one cause of magi death?" asked Professor Darvek, his hands outstretched to the class in invitation of a response.

"I disagree with the premise of your question as stated, professor," said Tobias.

Some of my classmates shuffled uncomfortably. Tobias occasionally showed up to class and his appearances were seldom graced with subtlety, nor did he forget to don vivid and lustrous raiment.

"Very well, then, Tobias," said Darvek. "Please elucidate to the class, in which you are not enrolled, I will remind you, the deficit in my query as posed."

"The textbook answer which it is apparent you are searching for is *wasted mana*," continued the dusty-haired, small but imposing mage just about a year older than myself.

"This fact is in reference to the statistic that between eight and nine out of ten instances in which a mage perishes in combat, they have already run out of mana, as would b- " said Tobias, continuing, until Trisha interjected.

Trisha stabbed her finger into the air towards him with rapid successions, each poke accentuated with green fire and sparks which matched the infuriated emerald of her eyes. She took her role as a teacher's assistant rather seriously, too seriously for some of my peers' likings. It was one of the few aspects of her character that I did not find distasteful.

"Which is why Professor Darvek is in this very lesson

hoping to emphasize wast-" said Trisha, seething.

"Waste not your breath on me, fair siren, I shall stand by my assertion," said Tobias, dismissing her with a mocking flick of his wrist. "In many of those eight or nine cases death was inevitable, either because of the difference in the quality, or the quantity, of opponents."

I remembered something my father told me when I was a little girl. He was scolding me because I had told him about how another classmate at school was being bullied because she couldn't use Bubblebreath. I didn't say anything because, like the other kids, I was afraid she would push me onto the floor with Windblast.

"It is only in moments worthy of fear that just actions are courageous, Ay." I remember his shaggy red hair, and his beard. There was always a wildness to my father's hair, except for his beard, which he kept precisely trimmed except for around Yesteryear, our magi Christmas and New Years combined. I recalled reaching up to him on the tips of my toes until he picked me up, and I told him that I would be braver next time.

"Even if loss or death is inevitable," I said, somewhat unsure of myself, "saving your mana could mean saving your Confluence... or your family... or someone's child. If death is inevitable, it's about what you can accomplish despite that fact."

Tobias paused for a moment, opened his mouth to speak, and then stopped. With a playful head tilt in acknowledgement of defeat, he said "I suppose."

Tobias bowed the specific bow the angle of which connotes a matrimonial pairing, to Trisha, and then looked at me, and smiled, and warped away in a flash of fire. It was moments like that afternoon that made me joke with Tobias about his declaration of me not being his enemy. I sheepishly received the glaring look of jealousy that Trisha prepared for me on most occasions on which Tobias and I interacted. Irrespective of the less than noble manner in which Tobias treated Trisha, she felt a bitter possessiveness towards him. She absolutely despised the fact that Tobias and I explored Somnumes. He ignored all of the invitations in which she offered for the two of them to partake together.

Do not waste mana. I repeated the four words in my mind like a mantra as I reflected on the situation, and remembered that memory. I was on an island of indeterminate size. There was an increasingly ominous storm blowing steadily away from the distant horizon and towards my current position. I trembled with fear. I felt the dizzying lack of a heartbeat as a soreness in my chest. I looked up to the skies which were inching towards the burst of sunset before darkness, and I was sweating profusely. I nearly succumbed to dread.

An inner voice, with a regal confidence which resonated with mystic power, as if the sound itself wore armour made of glass and gold... told me to close my eyes. I listened.

"O' Lioness of Light, O' Effulgent One, as surely as wind unerringly bends waves, you are a kindled spirit. How then have you found yourself tethered as such with unneeded trepidation? Within what imagined glass encasement, forged of sands of self-doubt, have you bound yourself? Rolling like a kitten's long-ago-unravelled wool, to-and-fro, here and there, there and here. Surely it is by humility, and not negligence, that you have forgotten that direction of Ascension. Open your heart and shed all occlusions of worry; for the peaks of your path are all punctuated upwards."

My eyes were still closed. I kept my heart open against the tightness of breathless fear. There was dread on the horizon, and

143

there was embodied void that simmered beneath my consciousness. I grasped it with my being and held it in place as though it was a red-hot coal. Letting go, I knew quite well, would bring about calamity. Ignore it. And with earnest effort, with a spirit emboldened by words I found calming, I brought my open hands together and bowed slightly as I closed my eyes.

I rested my mind's eye on a peaceful energy, and I expanded my consciousness in a radial sphere until my perceptions included all of the island, and only the island. Once again, I heard the chrrrrrr of the wind. The increasingly sinister cyclone chipped away at the safety offered by the distance between us. The skies were a confused smearing of watercolour sunset and putrid greens, malevolent fuchsias, foreboding dark greys, and multi-coloured cloud-to-cloud lightning. The lightning illuminated the vapor with demonic iridescence.

With hands clasped, I warped without knowing my destination. I was guided by poorly-understood but obeyed 'intuition'. I opened my eyes and found myself at the top of a large rocky hill, the crest of the tropical island. It was from this vantage point that I observed that there was not one island, but an archipelago - island triplets. If there was anywhere I would find W.B and Harold, it was on one of the other two islands. But they were too far to warp to. I had to find them and the three of us needed to get out of here. My heart held a knowing fear that this encapsulated realm was not to be trifled with.

I pondered what was available to me on the island, and I walked over to a coconut tree, and I rested my hand on the rough trunk. I felt a grumble in my stomach. With a come-hither motion, I detached a few coconuts and levitated them towards me. I 'dissolved' my hand into energy with Phaseshift, pushed into the first coconut, and absorbed the energy directly into my spirit. It may interest you to know that, despite ordinary taste and digestion being skipped, there was a purity and a coconut-ness to the coconut. I was satiated, and somewhat replenished, after I finished absorbing my third.

Even after my partial replenishment, those islands were certainly too far for me to try warping across the water in my current condition. How would I get to them? What could I do? I leaned against the coconut tree, and was quite alarmed to hear a sharp crack, and a moment later, a crashing sound. A withered palm frond loosened by the increasing wind had fallen right beside me. I reached out and touched the faded, rough frond and wondered how long it had been waiting to fall. I turned and looked up at the top of the trees, and there was a sensuous loveliness to the way that the palm leaves flowed in the steadily increasing wind.

An idea popped into my head, a semi-blurry image, the rough sketch of a solution to my problem. Okay, I'm going with it. I levitated towards me green leaves and cuttings from each of the trees around me until I had enough. I energized the floating leaves with the frequency needed to phaseshift them, and fused them into a completely smooth sheet of tropical green. Three yarn-thin, but stronger-than-spider-silk cords of mana bonded against the flapping sheet of leaf. The three cords thickened into one thicker ring of mana which wrapped around my wrist. The sail danced behind me. It was like a giant kite on a bracelet.

After turning to face the next island, I channelled Lightswift and dashed forward, and with my blurry speed, I jumped off the cliff. Mid-air, I extended an extra cord of mana to bind myself to the sheet with a second handle. Using the resistance of the wind to guide me, over a half-second, I oscillated the shape of the plant-based cloth until the geometries served my aerodynamic intentions. I kited down across a canopy forest onto the grey shore with the sand freckled with specks of red metal. I pulled together the husks from palm fronds around me and energized them before redistributing the material into a surfboard-esque panel. Another light swift, and I jumped up, magically balancing the board, and keeping it lined-up beneath my feet. I amplified the strength of the board, like a layer of fortifying glaze. I heard the crash of the board against the sea. The sail caught the wind and I shot forward towards the nearest island.

The cyclone had mutated into something truly grotesque. The twisted bands of deathly clouds were visibly rotating, and the spinning was getting faster. The winds were blowing stronger. The dreadful storm was accelerating on its path towards the archipelago. It almost felt as if I was in a wind tunnel, such was my swiftness combined with the gusts of storm as my makeshift kite-raft propelled me onwards. I struggled to keep my eyes open against the oncoming salty mist. It stung my eyes. The gusts seemed to cut at my skin. The ocean was choppy. Here and there I glided off a medium-height wave, and crashed down onto the water as I kept moving forward.

I made it to the front of the other island, and as I did so, branches of the massive storm exploded outwards. The bands of cloud rapidly encircled the archipelago with a perimeter of dreadful, demonic clouds. Over a dozen tornadoes (these looked more terrifying than your typical waterspout) rotated like undulating columns of void energy. They sucked up the water and were occasionally illuminated by flashes of red and green and yellow lightning. Around the edge of the ring of clouds, torrential rain began pouring down. Incredible gusts burst the droplets into explosions of mist. Facing the island, a blob of grey cloud the size of a few houses pushed together, descended from the cloud tops. Dark eye-like pits formed and deepened.

A mouth formed, a black recession, no teeth. The mouth opened and blasted out lightning which went in every direction; some bolts arced back into the clouds. Other bolts blasted trees on the island. I saw at least four trees burst into flames which were quickly extinguished by rain. A couple exploded. A single purple and red lightning bolt blasted to within an inch of my feet. It spiralled up around me without touching me like a pasta-swirl of arcane-coloured electricity.

Coming from the opposite direction, I saw W.B pull a tornado towards her before freezing the bands into a vortex of shards of ice. She bent the frozen tornado and skated across it towards the face of the Voidlord. Right as she got in front of the face, she burst open the twisting column of dagger-sharp ice, creating an explosion of frozen dust. She was trying to break apart the winds in her efforts to significantly weaken the entity.

The cloud being laughed. The deepness of the voice was like the thud of a marble pillar being lifted and dropped up and then back down onto the ground. The hair on the back of my neck and arms stood up. At first, I thought it was fear, and then I realized it was the result of magically-amplified electric charge. All of the rain, which was now covering most of the sky, turned instead from water to icy dust in a spontaneously-created blizzard. But this occurred at the will of Hydroxis, who was using its mastery of weather to mock her.

The Voidlord emanated its thoughts which manifested as an all-pervasive sound which came from all directions. The deepness of its voice made the sand vibrate: "It is not by breath of wind that atmosphere is tempered. In no droplet's hands shall you find clasped the reins of my ever-storming fury. Your inscribed ice is as meek to me as a crushed insect is meek in the face of the Gods to whom your mountains pray. Live then in perpetuity, and be assimilated into my undying storm."

A few ice tornadoes departed from the ridge of clouds and shot towards Blizzard and knotted around her like frenzied, behemoth snakes of ice. The rapidly-spinning ice vortexes shifted and then tightened as a sphere of violet and red energized wind. Like the clouds, it was periodically illuminated by the flashes of multi-coloured lightning. The colossal sphere levitated up and zoomed towards the entity from which the wind had originated. Her defeat took under a minute.

W.B's assimilation was interrupted by Harold Hardbub, who with a precisely-powered three-dimensional matrix of individual void bursts, dispersed the enveloping mass of windy death.

I warped up into the air (a difficult feat, as it is not a typical ability of the aura to directly lift itself), and caught Blizzard. I wrapped one arm around her and wrapped a band of mana around her like a belt, to keep her tethered. It would be inaccurate to say that we glided down, because really we almost crashed. But I did succeed in softening our landing onto the grey sand shore. There was no way I could risk trying to warp, and accidentally exploding, Madison's mother. I looked down at her face. The darkness of her skin had faded from chocolate tones to dull and lifeless. Instead of a snowstorm in her eyes, there was only a light blue. Her body was warm. For a mage who had tattooed her body as a signature for the Guardian Angels of ice… W.B's warmth was a terrible sign.

Hydroxis laughed a God-like laugh that made pebbles on the sand jostle; tendrils of static electricity sizzled across the sand of the island and tickled my skin without shocking me. It was as if Hydroxis was an electric sun contemplating the taste of our bodies. Harold warped over next to us and touched W.B's skin, and gasped in shock. Harold projected a barrier field around the three of us. The small dome of his mana had the faint smell of lamb and rosemary. It is said that the nearest and dearest thing to a Hardbub's heart, is their stomach.

Amplifying his voice, Harold said, "Voidlord! I am the Grand Magister of the United Magisterium, and I have not yet authorized the assimilation of my soldier. Where is the paperwork? Identify yourself, *immediately.*"

I turned and looked at Harold as if to say, "What the fuck are you doing?", but he turned and opened his eyes wide as if to tell me to "shut the fuck up."

The many tornadoes, which shifted from ice back to deathly winds, tilted to the side in obvious confusion. I heard an odd sound and sensed Harold projecting towards Hydroxis a messy blur of bureaucratic nightmares. He was trying to out-dread a Voidlord.

"This is the second and final instance in which I shall inquire as to your preferred title, you windy cretin," continued Harold, rising with confidence as he walked outside his barrier.

The clouds shrivelled slightly, the tornadoes grew ever so slimmer, and the Voidlord stuttered as he told us his name was "Hy-Hydroxis".

"Battlemage Aylene," roared Harold. There was a wild gusto in his voice, and his wide frame was somehow imposing even despite the being of death beside us. "Bring forth the paperwork, immediately."

Harold began to warp me into a salute but I finished his positioning and conjured a stack of rough paper. The texture was at least partially inspired by the coconut tree husk. I marched forward across the sand with an air of military seriousness.

"Grand Magister, sir! In accordance with Article Fifty-Seven... Cloud, Part II, I have prepared for you the paperwork pertaining to the assimilation of a Mrs. Walking Blizzard, Arcane Guard, Rank Blue Alpha."

"Tell me, Hydroxis, and that is of course assuming you have mustered the courage to properly identify yourself, you windy ruffian," hissed Harold with convincing indignation, "does that *sound* like the title of a mage with whom a foggy fool ought to be trifling with?"

The tornadoes stiffened up, as if reminded of their potency through this moment of disrespect. *"I AM HYDROXIS, EMPEROR OF STORMS, IT IS BY MY MALEVOLEN-"*

Harold amplified his voice even further and interrupted Hydroxis. "Is your boisterousness part of your ill-intended efforts to impress me, you cloudy wretch? You regard yourself with the power of a God and yet you falter at the shadow of the thought of signing the necessary paperwork to complete your task. I offer you my *pen.*"

Our equivalent to a president conjured a palm tree sized pen-like pillar (I sensed him dematerialize a tree some ways behind us to conserve energy), and levitated it up towards the being.

I am quite unsure as to which of the three of us was the most baffled at this encounter. Was it myself, unnerved and impressed at the gall of my nation's leader, or was it my leader's surprise at his ploy working? It did indeed seem to be the deftly-befuddled manifestation of void.

"If you have the faintest inkling of a shadow of an outline of a consciousness," said Harold, "surely you can see the utensil before you. Surely you can accomplish this meagre task. Go on then, pick it up, and with haste. I have important matters to attend to."

The hurricane's face pushed forward with concerted effort. A tornado snaked down towards us before splitting into three micro-vortexes, each the size of my body, as it attempted to pick up the... writing utensil. Harold levitated the palm tree pen and swooshed it around through the air, making it quite difficult for the increasingly frustrated entity to firmly grasp it.

The hurricane blackened with fury, as if on the verge of comprehending our deception. "Vehement one, you task me with an impossible task. How can I grasp that which is ever-moving?"

"A-hah! Your humility is well-received, Hydroxis," said Harold, waggling a finger. "Before I answer, I must convey to you a humility of my own. I know not what this field is through which this pen is ever-moving. Have you pondered this mystery? What is this invisible thing by which the waves of water are stirred?"

The hurricane seemed to crouch forward, unsure of itself, dipping its head before bobbing up with giddy excitement. "...Wind? Is it wind? *I am HYDROXIS, THE STORMING FU-*"

I almost peed myself.

"Brilliant!" said Harold, squeaking with delight, his hand slammed against my shoulder in a forceful gesture of support. "Absolutely brilliant. I've spent a handful of eons trying to decipher that nasty detail. You know what an eon is, don't you?"

Hydroxis, bewildered, deflated as a network of lightning bolts pondered this query. "Eons... eons... yes. I know of eons. I have known many."

"Then I have one question remaining, and it does seem to me to be a rather important one," said Harold. "And do you know what it is? Do you care to know?"

Silence. Absolute silence.

"I will take from you that silence, you cumulo-nincompoop. How could ever it be that an 'emperor of storm', whose very breath can break islands, how could such a being be stopped by lowly wind? Surely the stars are impervious to being burned by candles, nor the ocean drowned by a droplet. Upon reflection, it is clear to me that it is only by *arrogance* that you regard yourself a storming fury," Harold sighed with feigned disappointment. "It is regrettable, but I now know you to be *less* than the omitted error of an accidentally calculated fraction of a neglected summer breeze. Poor thing! Neither fierce, and certainly not lovely enough to compel childhood delight. Ah well, send us on our way, and with haste, lest I spirit ether these papers to your faded vigour, and condemn you to eons of searching and never signing."

Silence. Hydroxis and Harold stared at each other. Harold's face projected an air of superiority and the utmost disdain.

With the slow rhythm as if each syllable was an allusion to a guillotine, Harold spoke. "I will be the storm in your soul, Hydroxis. I will be your abacus, and I will count for you each eon."

The hurricane, Hydroxis, shrank until it was not much larger than an SUV as it floated towards us meekly.

"Such severity shall not be necessary, O' Nightmare," said Hydroxis, whose voice was stuttering with fear. "If it would please you, I will escort you from this stillness of wind that is my lowly abode. O' Nightmare, I am not in need of punishment. I offer you my guiding breeze. Please blanket me with your zephyr mercy, and I will oblige all that you ask of me."

And so it came to be that a trembling typhoon obliged us in our desire to depart its realm. With wavering winds, Hydroxis opened the gate in the fabric of its encapsulated reality, and guided us with a terrified gentleness from its Umbrume abode. We passed through the embedded non-reality of a single book to a realm of interwoven realities and antirealities. We crossed into Cosmoria.

Chapter 20

Hustlesprouts, A Tale of Hardbub

There is a legend-or-truth which usually, but not exclusively, is recited by a Hardbub, and to a Hardbub, in accordance with the goals of one or more Hardbubs. You may think to question as to how frequently could such a story, involving such persons, be told? The answer would perhaps surprise you, for the Hardbub family is quite sprawling, and we are rich in tradition, or else our tradition is sensory richness. Enmeshed with an inherited predisposition for appetite and charisma is the Hardbub proclivity for, and efforts directed towards, gastronomical delights, and fights enliquored.

It is not altogether uncommon that two perceptive Hardbubs, be they cousins or sisters or brothers either knowingly or unknowingly (we have been a... prosperous... people), stumble upon the same forest scavenge able (useful, valuable, or most importantly, delectable) thing. This is only problematic when the instance-of-detection between the two or more Hardbubs is close enough for doubt. Or if particularly heavy-set or other similarly-incapacitated Hardbubs, still passionate regarding their pursuit, make off for the same boon. My father's second cousin, twice removed, had to transfer to a layperson college after attempting to publish a semi-satirical research paper containing a predictive model related to the age, weight, hunger and arm-hair texture of the Hardbubs involved in a given dispute.

Our excessively recited legend-or-truth is related to that archetypical family conflict. It is the story of one of our matriarchs, Heather Hardbub, to whom we attribute the discovery of Hustlesprout. It is semi-common layperson knowledge that broccoli, brussels sprouts, cabbage, cauliflower, kale and quite a few other household vegetables come from the same plant. Less known is that Hustlesprout is the long-forgotten ancestor of that entire family. Each of those sub-varieties were but an eventual offshoot from that original source of unbridled, golden-and-pink, fuzzied, leafy crunch.

There was, our story goes, a relatively large Hardbub clan which occupied a prosperous forest village somewhere or other in Medieval Europe. This particular branch, with their prosperity and their multiplicative affinities, entered a period in which the collective family's gourmand endeavours had left the forest devoid not of edible food, but of desirable food. Increasingly scarce morsels, the long-fabled Forest Jewel Crab. The hunted-to-extinction Moon Deer, unceremoniously slurped Honeyslugs... I could go on for some time. Our family's records certainly do, as of early 2020, two hundred and seventy-eight species that were formerly consumed are now extinct.

The political machinations that ensued after the onset of the Medieval epicurean drought would have frightened Machiavelli.

But the Hustlesprout, with its latent ability to greatly increase confidence, mood and most especially desires for entrepreneurship, saved our people. Heather discovered the technique needed to correctly cultivate Hustlesprout, which is extremely rare in the wild, and is notoriously finicky in its growth. She used it and then set up a trade network by which we amassed a fortune of worldy-exchanged magi spices and other delicacies. Alongside our rise to prominence, glass coins with their hollows filled with dried Hustlesprout became the de facto magi currency of the era, hustlebubs. We have enjoyed a lengthy, ongoing period of economic prosperity, with only rare intermissions, although our currency was eventually replaced by the less flavourful fiat currency, the enchanted-to-avoid-replication Scrigget.

Chapter 21

A Fondly-Regarded Pepper

Lofty ambitions are not at all uncommon amongst our people; indeed, it seems some people are cursed by the knowledge of our lacking our ancestor's wings. Magiphysicists, ever-puzzled by their perpetually-evolving science, have a running joke regarding flight which I first heard recently. It is as conveyed, if not in words precisely, quite thoroughly in spirit.

"In what manner might a mage manage flight?" asks the joke-teller.

"Relieve me of my curiosity," or something similarly frivolous, is a typical response.

"By an elixir, meticulously brewed!" concludes the jokester, perhaps with a hiccup and a sarcastic, "Thank ye' O' Light!"

Collective transitions from sobriety to liquored lofts tend to ensue thereafter. As erroneous as binary splits during moments of philosophical musings usually are, it has often been said that there are two kinds of magi: those who enjoy varied and frequent elixir, and those who are boring. We do not drink to remember, nor do we drink to forget our comrades dismembered. The magi have our Demons, and we imbibe for borrowed peace. There are whiskies which add a reddish sparkle to the world around you, like cherry soda splashed against your glasses. There are wines which enhance charisma, and to clarify, this is a significant addition further above the baseline reduction of inhibitions.

As it turns out, Riverkiss is in fact a real elixir. Studies indicate that for over ninety-five percent of adult magi, Riverkiss enables the remote sensing of all amphibians within a spherical radius. The magnitude of the radius correlates proportionally to the mass of the primer used in brewing. Despite the name, this is primarily used for gastronomical and ecological purposes, as opposed to amorous inclinations.

The exquisite Stormeye Rum is what I have found myself quite drawn to; it has been a sublime respite in the face of our current great sufferings. I quite enjoy the drink of turquoise, with all of its blue fizz. As one gulps it, the flavours shift and roll and peak with the natural variance of waves slamming against a shore. I have secured myself an appreciable supply, and I am learning to brew it myself; the ingredients for the fermented elixir are as follows:

1. One pound of flesh of the Cocothotte Tree, which can be identified by the three varied personalities on the triad coconut Spirit. It is said that the shriek of agony upon the plucking of the first coconut, on most occasions, succeeds in preventing the taking of the other two. It is for this reason recommended that all three coconuts are severed simultaneously, or that the harvester is deaf.

2. Four cups of Seaquartz Crab Oil of a crustacean of at least twenty years of age. It is a fortunate thing for this crab that its replenishable oil increases in quality as it grows older. The crab itself is said to be a rather unique delicacy, though it is quite rare as they are difficult to farm, and the oil is more profitable. The oil, drunk alone and in sufficient quantity, aqueforizes the body for a few hours. This leaves the imbiber able to breathe underwater, and surge through any crevice in their aqueous form.

They become energized liquid and this has its uses, as you can imagine. Incidentally, this is one of the most powerful ways to survive any of a great variety of poisons. The poison droplets can be squeezed out with a hearty puff.

3. One tablespoon of powdered Dream Salt, the fineness of which is extremely important for a consistent brew. Coarser chunks have resulted in unpleasant but non-fatal side effects in the imbibing connoisseur. Ironically, Dream Salt makes it impossible to sleep until the effect wears off, but it adds a dreaminess to the world. It softens the glow of lights, and it muffles the textures of that which you see, touch and hear, all senses. It is quite frequently used by magi in Goa on the Indian subcontinent.

4. One Whistle Pearl, the size does not generally matter. This is actually not the most expensive ingredient, as over the last two centuries the Oistashuk yields have increased significantly as the coastal farmers refined their techniques. Note that the pearl only actually "whistles" when you touch it whilst it is immersed in warm water. These decrease slightly in size and loudness after each batch and one pearl can generally be used for at least eight to ten brews. After enough uses, the colour shifts to brown, and the taste added is abhorrent.

5. Five tablespoons of dried Dragonmoss Mint. This is by far the rarest ingredient, as Water Dragons typically only surface once every twelve to fifteen years. The moss grows like thick seaweed down from their stomachs. It is a symbiotic relationship where the plant absorbs nutrients from the ocean water as the Dragon travels. In return, the plant secretes pheromones which attract fish. Note that Dragonmoss Mint must *only* be consumed after being fermented. It is extremely toxic while raw, and one tablespoon is enough to kill three adult males, or one Hardbub of

158

any gender. This is the primer in this mixture, and the other ingredients, except for the cane sugar juice, are amplicants.

6. Eighteen cups of thickened cane sugar juice. This is the only ingredient that is also known and used by the laypeople. Other carbohydrates can be used instead, but this is the sugar with which this elixir has the most potency and flavour synergy.

My nervousness is such that only Stormeye Rum has been able to calm my nerves to any non-negligible degree. I am stoic in the face of our people, but I find my thoughts meandering, and I am stricken with grief. Our people are on the brink of a civil war that has erupted nearly over night, and I feel nearly helpless in my ability to prevent it. The Raconds have demonstrated their resolve to defend Tobias and fight his persecution. They claim that Aylene's disappearance alongside father and Walking Blizzard is ample evidence that he should be exonerated. Our laws are rather unmalleable, and Racond resistance has charged the political atmosphere.

Rumours of the Umbrume and Marvin, Tobias and Aylene leaked from the Arcane Guard into the general public. It seems that all of the magi have already decided on which of the two they rest their faith, and the other is the worst of villains. Racond is a member of a *current* Great House, and the furious Draconic flames of the Racond family have protected our people with the incineration of thousands of Demons. Their position is that it was the Candent family who was dishonoured, and stripped of their royalty, and it was obviously Aylene who had defiled her oath. No one has seen Tobias, and adding to the tension is another rumour that a mage in the Arcane Guard had executed him in lieu of bringing him to Lunaris.

The Tornetts, Kerbens, and the Chereks have officially sided with the Raconds. Obviously, we Hardbubs and our allied Von Bears are with the Candents, and we are backed by the Kekonzulu and Raj'pathanis. The desert clans, who are satellites of the Candents and Kandenthakans, are particularly riled up. They are quite vocal in their defending of Aylene's character. The Ma'jents and Dentari have already expressed their willingness to go to war against the Raconds, and, if anything, it appears they are foolishly eager. The Hardbubs are not so eager for fratricidal catastrophe.

The desert tribes adamantly believe Aylene should not be castigated or judged on account of her father's selfish action; he has already perished. His death was the fair and whole punishment in accordance with law and scripture. The Candent family, with their ostracization and loss of status and wealth, has already suffered immensely for a decade. They would not tolerate any more mistreatment towards Aylene.

Uncle Henrik has, in my father's absence, found himself in a leading position within the Wing Council. Osmidius, Tobias' grandfather, is his primary political adversary. He is also amongst the most powerful of all the magi alive. There are maybe ten mages around the world in the same tier of power level. He is orders of magnitude mightier than the majority of magi; his usage of Pyrence has been measured and found to exceed a one-mile radius. We Hardbubs are working rather earnestly to avoid a war.

I have left the Academy and have taken my place alongside my family. I am advocating for peace and patience. My internal interests are obvious to those privy to my affections. Despite this, I have exercised discretion and fairness in my discourse with the Raconds and Tornetts. A potential solution to this conflict was discussed as holding in captivity both individuals, until such time that the truth of the matter could be determined. Who would be doing this determining, and the precise nature of this methodology, was a group of details omitted. It was the less fiery-tempered of the nation's leading elite who suppressed the flames of war to dangerous embers.

But there is a weakened forest, and there is kindle wood aplenty. We like to believe in and loudly proclaim our solidarity, such is the way of the magi. But our hearts have been quite heavy since the void bomb earlier this year. There is still a great uncertainty as to whose negligence in particular allowed for that to occur. It has for some time been widely known that the barrier around Lunaris, and the boundaries between Earth and Da'raakan, will dissipate within a year. It seems this mortal anxiety is manifesting as political posturing. The electric charge of the thought of death has, like lightning, polarized our people.

Just as many of our classmates back on campus do, I quite often find my thoughts resting on you, Aylene.

I speak regularly with Madison, who is quite eager to know both of your and her mother's whereabouts and well-being. The semester has ended, and Marvin is back at home recovering; we think he'll be back in the spring. The harm offered onto Marvin, which he himself knows increasing fragments of, has leaked out as whispered rumours.

It is firmly enshrined, crystalized as if sand forged with God's light, that we do not give way to fear of darkness. It is not simply murder, it is tantamount to a divine treason, it is the greatest defilement of our blessings. For light to slay light when there is a universe of unending shadow that seeks to envelope us, when our existence is at war with hungering calamity, is unthinkable. I know it was not you, Aylene. I know how resolute you are in your quest for redemption.

You may have blundered, but you did not commit this mortal

sin. Aylene, I maintain for the thought of you a brave face, and a heart full of optimism. I know that you are with my father and Walking Blizzard, and I believe you are safe. You are likely hearing the all-too-often repeated stories my father Harold is infamous for; there is a joy in them as recited. You will come to know the events therein as ever-increasingly embellished, though I do miss them, and him, myself.

In speaking forthrightly, I find myself quite in longing of a reciting of a song as emitted by the voice of my light, loved. Aylene; your fieriness is a capsaicin missed dearly. It may interest you to know that I am making unusually swift progress in the cultivation of your future namesake pepper. You are my music, and my heart, and I miss you as the shore misses the low tide ocean.

There are your emblazoned scarlet locks which grow redder with emotional charge. I miss your eyes of ruby and amber for which your family is famous. I frequently find myself missing the contrast between my sun-sheltered self and your flame-kissed darkness. You have a noble lineage, and you bear no mark in my eyes on account of your father's actions. With your frequent place in my thoughts, I often muse that in another life I encountered you by happenstance. Or else I hold this hope quite dearly, for the prospect of your forever-absence is a cold shadow, unacknowledged but firmly within my periphery.

Under normal circumstances, even with my less-than-exceptional prowess, I can distinguish your aura from a mile away as easily as I can detect a truffle on a nearby plate. In truth I have no hunger but for the cessation of this despair, a reprieve from this not knowing. How can I be both optimistic, yet also tortured? I do not know. I feel myself enveloped in a storm, and yet I enjoy the peace of the centre. But this is perhaps the increasingly frequently present effect of the Stormeye Rum. It seems I have succumbed and am further succumbing to my family's propensity. We are so close to a civil war, Aylene. I hope, and we all need, for the three of you to return soon. Our people are a red-hot needle poorly-balanced on a finger of death; we are a half-breath from destruction. It is as if we have foolishly forgotten about the void which seeks to consume us. With serendipity, may the merciful Mother's benevolent gaze grace us with victory, and hope. God speed, Aylene. By my faith I know you'll save us all.

Chapter 22

Cosmoria, Realm of Realms

I felt the increasingly-familiar sensation of interdimensional dissipation as I transitioned out of Hydroxis' abode, and into Cosmoria. My eyes were closed as the pulsing accelerated, and I felt at my core the outline of embodied void. It was like a blob of darkness inside my chest which periodically sparked flicks of shadow, as if it was testing my resolve. It wished to escape, and I had the worrisome, ongoing sense that it doing so would result in catastrophe. I clenched my energized fists, my eyes were closed, and I pushed down the shadow, compressing it into a small sphere the size of a marble.

Alongside each flick of shadow, I felt micro-pulses of the void energy surge through my dematerialized body. It didn't hurt at all; if anything, it was replenishing. Our oscillation ceased as our corporeality started finalizing its manifestation in a plane of Cosmoria. In front of me I saw the wide, energized frame of Harold Hardbub. His grandness of spirit radiated warmth and confidence. Next to him, I sensed Walking Blizzard. Her frosty inclinations were conveyed as a radiance which, if you focused on it, felt like a perfect gust of cold on an otherwise hot autumn day.

There was a winter in the frigid flow of her aura. But I also felt occasional flickers in her energy, brief moments where instead of her pleasant cold, there was a sickly, hot and anxious feeling. I placed my hand on W.B, and without me casting a healing incantation, a wave of amplified mana surged out of me and coursed into her aura. Blizzard's aura burst outwards in a frosted, wintery puff of snowflakes and frozen dust. She exhaled relief, as if she were taking a sudden gasp after nearly drowning.

We turned and examined our surroundings. In the sky, there was an array of ethereal planets which glowed with supernatural neons like dye-filled marbles of crystallized fire. If you looked up at them, you felt them tug at your being. It was immediately apparent that too long of a stare would result in your assimilation.

In the 'atmosphere' above us, like the ocean between those cosmic Demon planets, there were rapidly moving, distinctly-coloured auroras of gradients of turquoise, citrine, lilac, and carnelian. It was as if the coloured skies had been divided into armies of enchanted lines waging war against each other. Aurora-esque streaks of coloured energy would lurch forward and surround lines of other colours like a coiled snake, wrapping around the prey it would strangle. Then a third colour, or a third and the fourth at the same time, would flash through and obliterate the entangled mess. Or the two or three struggling gradients would cross through each other and attack in aggressive loops. The sky was eating itself, infinitely so. The chaotic flux in perpetuity is a defining characteristic of Cosmoria.

"This is where the Noc'raakan sent me," I said, astonished, as I looked around and found myself in a meadow of silver and black foliage, but with the familiar skies.

"This is what we have referred to as Cosmoria," said Harold, slowly. "A sea of dreams, or more often, nightmares; the network through which the ever-seeping blood of void seeks to permeate, and bring cessation to, our noisy existence."

165

As Harold spoke, I felt the marble-sized sphere of void energy inside my chest expand outwards and then contract in, as if angered by his words. For the first time, I became keenly aware that this presence was not unnoticed by Harold or Walking Blizzard. My soul was laid bare for them, in perfect parallel to the transparent familiarity of their spirits. The entity of void fizzed as if I were a volcano digesting a boulder. It was this quasi-mass of voidlessness that fuelled my cosmonuclear fire.

My emotional charge radiated outwards, and Harold and W.B spiritwatched how Tobias and I deceived Marvin through the perspective of my own past perception. They saw my sin I had tattooed myself with, as permanent a mark as Walking Blizzard. But my engraving was not dedication, it was manipulation. It was not courage, it was my mark of deception. My actions had subjected an innocent person to an infinity minus one of suffering, times infinity. The minus one just implies that it ended. I didn't even know how we managed to escape. Oh Marvin, I'm so sorry.

I'm so sorry.

I averted their gazes and looked down in shame, as the fiery shadows within my aura flared.

After a pained sigh, and changing his tone to the stoic Hardbub I knew: "It is by my faith and optimism that I consider our circumstances to be auspicious, and not a preview of calamity. Lead on, Aylene, in accordance with your light."

I saw the 'meadow' around me, but I also felt an almost mist-thin infinite array of pixel-sized antirealities. There was an unbridled energy to this realm of realms which crackled like an infinity of pop rocks, like static on a cosmic radio. I walked forward, and they followed behind me, and the forested world around us dissolved into an unending constellation of blurry star

166

streaks which were as plentiful as raindrops in a monsoon. Our spirits blazed through the cosmos and anticosmos as we lightcrossed, once again in an energized form. Around us, popping into and out of existence like bubbles popping before they even appeared, was a menagerie of millions of different entities with terrifying features. They appeared on our periphery like embodied nightmares, but they disappeared just as quickly, shrinking after seeing our mental and spiritual resolve.

Some ignored us the way an alligator might ignore the wind, eyeing some other prospective prey. There were others which seemed to watch us, as if they were an echoed shadow, following us with each repeated flickering appearance. Disappearing and returning, we were stalked by galactic apparitions. We would move down this hallway of stars, that corridor, nooks, crannies, awnings and rooftops of a quasi-formless celestial-anticelestial expanse. Cosmoria is perplexingly both undefined and yet easy to navigate; the reason for you being there tends to remind you of your destination. I ignored the entities of shadow as I honed in on the directional tug, a sort of magnetic line that was hooked to my spirit. We pulsed through existence like blazing lasers, and we crossed galactic canyons backward and forward in time, simultaneously.

A grumble which seemed to make the cosmos around us vibrate made time stutter for a fraction of a moment. Such was the entity's power. The grumbling deepened, accelerated, and then the array of spectral light around us was no more. There was only a massive circle of absolute blackness with an accretion disk which resembled the Cosmorian aurora. The magnetic rope tugging at the shadow flame in my cosmonuclear soul had consumed us. We were enveloped mind, body and soul by a Noc'raakan.

167

Chapter 23

Consumed By Shadows

Black and purple grass-like plants canvased the field around me, and similarly nightmarish vines wrapped around and strangled jagged hills of white rock. It was a Cosmorian night. The horizon was the same perpetual war of energetic auroras. The cacophony of that forested place was a dizzying barrage of haunting birdsong, and the monstrous screeching and gurgling of unknown entities. It seemed that there were monsters busy eating. The stench of the air was an unsettling mix of ground-soaked blood, and the fragrance of varied moon-fed flowers. My pointed earshad razor-thin tips. They quivered as I heard a triumphant boyish roar from a familiar voice.

"Alianii," the voice was exuberant. "I caught one. The rune from the book worked perfectly. You gotta come check it out!"

I dashed towards my companion. My body was embodied shadow, the translucency of which reverberated between solid and wisp. I found myself in front of a young shadow form boy, with arms and face of void. The pronounced veins on his arms were a piercing silver. His eyes were like two shard-shaped crystals of platinum which rotated in the pits of shadow.

The boy was holding in his hands a small creature the size of a shoebox. It was a mushroom being with a wide, circular head that was coloured with swirls of light-green and brown. Its eyes were sky blue and coin-sized, and it was struggling fervently to escape the claws of void that pierced through its primitive clothes and into its skin. The mushroom puffed out reddish-orange spores to try and poison the attacker, but they only made the boy sneeze while laughing. It squeaked out horribly, trying to get help. My ears stiffened as I heard tiny feet push past each other, crunching on the grass and dirt beneath their feet. I turned my head sharply, and my vision went grey except for the life flames. There was the boy, the creature in his clutches, and the five tiny embers which belonged to the fungi souls which observed us from an unsafe distance.

"No need to be scared. I'm only going to consume you," said Navmir with giddy excitement as his mouth stretched open ravenously. There were rows and rows of fangs.

The mushroom spectators were horrified, and I watched them watch their companion be devoured. Tiny, pathetic squeaks of agony quickly ceased as puffs of increasingly-red spore dust sputtered out from forceful crunchings of the jaw-ravaged mushroom. I was offered some, when nearly none was left, but I felt a primal craving for the taste of a different meat. I closed my eyes and focused on and amplified my hearing, and way in the distance I heard the steady rhythm of a four-legged beast galloping.

I burst into my Dread wing form. I was a giant bat-like creature with four ears and four wings of dark violet, with skin of celestial blue with bulging, lustrous silver veins. If Navmir was a Moon shadow Kitten, I was a Noctrani Skytigress - I was wind-borne death. My four ears twitched and rotated as they searched, before they locked on to what became my prey.

"You coming, Navmir?" I asked. My normal voice was raspy, as much of my breath was being funnelled through nasal tubes which emitted soundwaves.

I was the soundscape I heard. I saw everything, if not in colour, instead in absolute resolution of texture. I could discern the shift in sound as wind curved around the horns of a Nocrastag as it leapt across a creek. Navmir, covered in spore dust and mushroom bits and fluids, jumped and dispersed into a small bunny-sized void flame as he leapt onto my back. My four wings flapped back and I shot into the air like a Gargoyle Hawk, soaring above the field. I only needed to flap occasionally; the winds were strong and kept me aloft. I watched the outline of my shadow slide across the illuminated-by-many-moons ground. All of my focus was on the sounds of the environment. There was so much noise, but I could filter it as easily as a child could pluck a solitary pebble from a bucket. I heard and pursued the almost imperceptible gallops of a faraway prey I knew to be particularly delectable.

I chased the whitish creature on my soundscape horizon. I amplified my echolocation and narrowed my focus as I flew towards it. I confirmed the species through the three horns that protruded from curves around its luminous face. The majestic beast turned towards me when it detected the sound of my wings cutting through the air, closing the distance. The Trikornak bellowed and took off in a frightened rush of appreciable haste. They were amongst the fastest of the beasts made of light.

My four clawed hands sunk into its flesh, slamming the elk-sized animal forward onto the ground. It struggled fiercely, even managing to flip itself over, and then it kicked me in the chest. It would have crushed my ribs had I been in my preferred humanoid body. I pinned it down again. Navmir jumped off and transformed from his void flame to his more-humanoid shadow form. He opened his mouth and lunged down to tear at the struggling creature, but I caught him with an outstretched tendril of energy. I held him in place.

"Your savagery is not in accordance with my whim," I said, whilst in the form of Alianii. "There is a finer grace to the tranquillity of quick silence."

I pulled back one of my clawed hands; three remained pinning the Trikornak's head and two of its limbs. I looked at it and noticed the golden eyes. They were quite fearful. My claws lengthened, and with one slash, I beheaded the creature. The silver blood which flowed and spurted outwards evaporated into metallic-shimmering mist after a few moments of air exposure. The fragrance of the mist was reminiscent of temple incense – the fancier temples, anyway. They had money for the outlawed goods. I repositioned myself and bisected the body. I was still in my bat-like form. I gutted the animal, and discarded the innards, most of which were devoured gluttonously by Navmir.

The boy of shadow jumped towards one of the more valuable cuts. One of my clawed hands flicked him away like a marble, or a booger. He landed with a 'd'oh' against some tree or other, dispersing into shadow fog before rematerializing and dashing forward in a canine-like form. As he made his way over, I finished cutting up the internally-bluish meat, with the silverish veins and blood. Two of my hands pulled bags of shadow out and the other two hands plucked the meat and placed them into specific bags. I was a methodical huntress.

I wasn't actually in the mood for Trikornak (I thought I was), but it didn't matter because I knew it'd fetch me a pretty price in the city. There were three regulars that would buy the meat from me for sure, if they were in town. Worst case scenario, I'd head over to Noc'talai Alley and cut a deal with Ji'jeek. The pink Reptoid kind of gave me the creeps, not that I have anything against Reptoids. It just seems he doesn't blink, not with any of his three eyes.

"Can I have one of the horns? Please, pretty please! What does it taste like? Is it crunchy?" asked Navmir, stretching out his clawed hands of shadow as he hopped with giddiness.

He was somehow still ravenous despite having had his fill, times five, between the innards and the mushroom fellow.

"If you can hold it for five seconds, pipsqueak," I said, laughing, as I dispersed and rematerialized in the more humanoid form of a Voi'danari (archaic: they who eat the void).

I tossed it to him, snickering, and he jumped into the air to catch it. He held it for half a moment before yelping as it dissolved through his hand and landed on the ground. Navmir scowled at me and grumbled, obviously displeased at my deception. He sat down and pouted as his hand coalesced.

"You're more than welcome to eat it, you know," I said, laughing as I patted him. "You might not survive, though!"

"Yeah, yeah. You've made your point. Can we go home, now? I have a stomach ache."

I bowed playfully and rummaged through the pockets on my Abyssal Armor. It was dyed primarily black with purple accents, though I could change its colour and shape. I withdrew a six-sided gold coin which featured an enthusiastically-smiling Reptoid. I'd be smiling too if I had a Warpstone business, with the prices that bastard charged. You'd think he'd give a gal like me a discount for being a loyal customer. Ah, well. Sometimes you don't feel like flying.

I snapped my finger and the swirling black and violet voidfire surrounded the coin, and I threw it into the air in front of us. As the void flames finished consuming the metal, a portal with an outline of swirling violet and reddish-yellow opened up.

At the top of the gateway was the tell-tale golden signature in fancy script. That's how you could tell if it was or wasn't a counterfeit. Most Warp stones are legit, or at the very least functional, though they occasionally send you to the wrong place. Usually somewhere shifty. But they're okay - they get the job done, if you're not afraid of rough crowds. Even so, a lot of folks aren't keen on taking a one in thirty or forty chance of being instantly annihilated, and those risqué nights were the old Alianii. I was wealthy enough for the convenience of authentic Warp stones.

Navmir and I walked through the portal and warped to the centre plaza of Noctrizek, a city the dreary frigidity of which I had always found quite welcoming. The same old grey stones with the chalk-reddish cement which barely held the place together. Papano still had his hustle with the dancing, music-making Living Skeletons near the main gate to the plaza. Papano's so old it's incredible; I think the only reason he hadn't already dissipated for good was that he was holding onto the hope of making it big. If it was up to him, there'd be a ribcage ensemble on every corner.

"Go meet up with the others. I have to make a few sales."

Navmir pouted and resolved his shadow form self to the small, blue-haired, blue-eyed fellow with his pale skin, and his tiny nose. He was still in the fluorescent blue hair phase. If I took him where I was going, he'd get eaten for sure. Those guys don't play, and the gals are arguably more frightening. The ladies there would probably snatch him up and keep him as a pet, fatten him up, maybe. The eventual indulgence would typically be topped with a pinch of Mavreki Void Salt. I made my way through the busy corridors of the charmingly-dull stone bricks - the cold night air kissed my cheeks better than my lovers of recent memory -

173

and the wind sang in whistles. Nowhere does the wind whistle her enshrouding song like Noctrizek.

"Alianii, is that you? Where are my Vantercrystal Boots? Don't you walk aw-"

The Pyranaki weapons and armour merchant waddled his ever-burning self over to me, scowling as he shook a Flame Elemental hand at me.

"Sorry, wrong Voi'danari," I said, turning my face away and slipping down an alley.

He and a few of his incendiary-inclined companions whooshed around looking for me. I dispersed into shadow and zoomed up the corner of an alley's end, and I rematerialized on the roof. I kept myself almost fully translucent, which isn't easy, I'll have you know. I kept on, whooshing from rooftop to rooftop as I made my way further from that district. I found an old friend sitting on a table at Banoni park, close enough to the many restaurants he frequented, some of which he owned.

"Manolo!" I said, my voice bright and cheery, which he always pretended to be irked by. "What are you doing here? Oh, I *always* forget how wonderfully small this city is."

"Yeah, okay, what d'ya want?" said Manolo, flipping over his golden-backed cards onto the marble table. "Can't ya see I'm in the middle of something?"

Manolo was a little shorter than my preferred height, and rather chubby. He kept his head shaved bald, and his orange eyes portrayed a fieriness I occasionally stoked. One of his games was maintaining the air that he was always busy. His role in his entrepreneurial endeavours involved only the occasional, unanticipated and shortly-lived fury of an unannounced inspection. The pumpkin-faced Gourdkin with whom Manolo was playing cards looked rather irritated that I had not introduced myself.

I mimicked Manolo's accent. "Ye' ye' ye, I know the deal, pal. I got the *product*, the good ol' silvah, with a bit of hooves if you know what I'm talking a-bout, yes sir. Fresher than blood honey off an Amor'ani's tummy."

I indulged a pleasant memory of a rather sensual encounter some nights ago, the aforementioned honey included. The Gourdkin with whom Manolo had been playing gasped, seemingly horrified. "If you are insinuating that you have in your possession the meat of a Trikornak, which is *highly illegal,* I am afraid that the only recourse is for me to report you to the appropriate authorities... if Dresha'kan were to find out... it would not be good. I can assure you of that, it would *not* be good!"

The Gourdkin slammed a hand of vine against the table. It was shivering with nervous energy and speaking with hasty exasperation. I remained silent, mildly curious to see if it would proceed with its unexcused-by-ignorance insolence.

"I do not much care for your impertinence, indifference, and your impropriety. Why, you didn't even greet me, you wretched poacher," continued the Gourdkin, with a foolish sense of empowerment which resulted from my silence. "I was top of my patch and here I am in this blasted city and everyone thinks they can waltz on over me and do *this*, and do *that*, and say *this*. N.O. No more! If we cannot find an adequate solution to this, I'm afraid I have no choice but to report you, and that will be that. Now if we were to share-"

"Manolo," I said, my voice sing-song, but my violet eyes blazing with death, "it does appear that your companion is new to this part of town. He has found it within himself to threaten me - twice, as a matter of fact."

"It is not a threat, it is most-assured. Of course, that is only if we cannot come to some sort of *agree-*" said the Gourdkin, as its final words were interrupted.

There is a certain pompous, vegetable-ness, Gourdkin-ness to the Gourdkins that has always succeeded in unveiling my temper. They are amongst my least favourite of the Vegenoids, though I own a farm which harvests them. My fury exploded and the Gourdkin was in one stroke of my cleaving claws obliterated into ready-for-sugar cream chunks of pumpkin flesh. Whoops! It happens to the best of us.

A handful of other Vegenoids at nearby tables at the restaurants and stores looked over, rather alarmed. One of the funny things about Vegenoids in general is that their nature as food generally eludes them. They understand rules, often rigidly so. They understand meat; some even like and get addicted to the taste of it. Even though they *can* explain where things come from, like a variety of flesh from a specific creature... they don't *comprehend* predation. They can describe the cause, and the effect thereafter, but something just doesn't click.

Someone back in the older night bred them as such; they were sold as companion beasts with "enhanced utilities". In seeing an unpleasant end to another similar being, Gourdkins do not develop a fear towards the cause of the other creature's end. Rather, they develop a usually-short-lasting anxiety that they too, arbitrarily, might cease to exist as if smitten by Dresha'kan's starbolt. It's kinda fucked up, but you can sing a Gourdkin a song about the pie for which it will be used as an ingredient. The little black-marble eyes will just look at you as if you asked a pebble two times two. Manolo sighed sadly as he wiped sticky strands of pumpkin flesh, seeds and all, off of his expensive-looking, garnet button-up shirt.

176

"I'm taking out double the costa' this shirt for me having ta' replace it, understand?" scowled Manolo, who was tearing up slightly. His outstretched hands gestured towards the now-more-colourful cobblestone ground. "Look at this mess. I was gonna' bake the little guy into a pie, it would've been beautiful."

"Who's to call that an impossibility, if you think about it. I saved you a bit of effort," I laughed a gentle laugh as I remembered a funny holiday memory.

Manolo rubbed his bald head in disbelief as he glanced around and assessed whether or not he could salvage any of the Gourdkin. He sighed more heavily, and his face quickly switched from shortly-lived sorrow, to apathy, to squinting at me in not-mild-but-medium annoyance.

"Sixty jeggies and not a gozet more, ya understand?" asked Manolo, as he pulled out a pouch and started counting the six reddish crystal coins, each worth ten jeggies, with each jeggie being worth one thousand gozets. Sixty thousand gozets, not bad for a quick hunt.

He handed them to me and I tossed all four of the large bags towards him simultaneously. He levitated them in the air, horrified at the thought that the bags might touch the cobblestone ground. The folks with the taste and means to cough up for Trika meat tend to treat it with the gentleness to keep it pure, at least until it's time for the Ash Ginger. I dashed forward and snatched a single gozet from his coinpurse, and he glared at me as he tucked the pouches into his ever-expansive satchel. Before he had the chance to get angry - well, angrier - I dashed forward and levitated in front of him one Trikornak Horn. I left it for him to keep as I re-joined the shadows of night. He had done plenty of favours for me, and every now and then I gave him a little token of appreciation.

As Manolo might say, "It ain't easy getting an Abyssal Whip."

He yelled out to me, quite obviously happy with the deal as transacted. "When you're coming back around here anyways? The gals down at Damenci's keep saying ya' gonna be the next big thing. Maybes even a Noc'raakan, heh."

Somewhere between never and now and a handful of back-again, I thought to myself. There was a part of me that disliked this attachment. It was certainly a non-negligible weakness. It is unbecoming of a Voi'danari to fear the silence of goodbye; there is no greater Honora to a place esteemed in one's heart. It is to love the perfection of that place, to choose to part, to hold it as once it was. As once it was in its most perfect of your moments. To crystalize it in time and pocket it, like a favourite gem, to later call upon in spirit in troubled times as needed. Goodbye, Navmir! Or maybe I'll see him unmorrow. I am, if anything, occasionally capricious.

Chapter 24

My Awakening

I felt myself being prodded with a stick. I looked up and saw a blue-haired boy standing on the other side of the cage. It took me a moment before I reacted. I was in a sort of muddled haze, and my body wobbled side to side slightly with my disorientation. In hindsight, I recall my hands being quite small. I looked around and saw other beings like me, also cramped in cages, though I was alone in a cage on my own. The adults' wings glowed orange and white and gold, but they were tied together around their backs so they couldn't open. The greenish metal with silver streaks burned my hands slightly as I held on to the bars and tried to break them. The pain was not enough to make me let go.

"Awwh. Take a look at the little red one," said a tall, well-figured and fancily-dressed woman with blood-red skin and yellow eyes with snake-like slits. "Her wings haven't even finished budding and she thinks she can escape."

A grey-skinned creature with yellow, frog-like eyes wiggled its three-fingered amphibian hands in delight. It was wearing an outfit even more ostentatious than the woman. His outfit gave him this snazzy-but-sleazy sort of look, like he was the eccentric owner of a murderers-and-thieves speakeasy in that vile Cosmorian city.

"Eighty jeggies and she's all yours, Miss Efrezek - seventy-five with a kiss on the cheek from a lovely like you." The merchant brought his hands together as he waddled closer to her. She towered above him.

"Oh, don't be silly, a lovely like *me*? What could you possibly mean by that?" The woman flipped her black hair to her other shoulder, rolling her eyes. "Why, Todeki, you little devil, you're only saying that because you like it when I buy your Alvish. I won't let you get me with the flattery this time." She wagged her finger at him, smiling playfully.

"Best I can do is seventy jeggies," he replied. "Less than that and the otha' fella's gonna take my ribs out for playing favourites. Ain't that right, boys?"

The various entities ranged highly in what degree their body format resembled anything remotely-human. They made various gestures that demonstrated the specific methodologies by which a rib-removing occurrence could shift from plausible to past-tense.

The obviously aristocratic Demoness shook her head, pouting, pointing a finger which ended in a painted-gold claw, towards one of the other cages.

"I'm really more interested in that one over there," she said. "Yes, that's the one. Notice the hair, and the eyes. I think that most handsome of fellows could very well be the little lady's father."

My heart sank, then I felt it beat twice with the force and the bum-bum rhythm of a drum. I turned towards the man the bitch was pointing at, and I saw him with his sun-kissed skin, like mine. His eyes were a very familiar reddish-amber, and a small shift in the angle of light changed the glow of their appearance to a fiercer scarlet. His hair was red like mine, and slightly wavy... though his was even longer than my own. His beard was

180

unkempt, and his hands were shackled together. He met my gaze and smiled at me, and mouthed to me that he loved me.

Some of the monsters gasped, some laughed, but the salesman proceeded with his business. "Shouldn't said handsome, Miss Efrezek, I knows your purse ain't all that shallow. See the shoulders? Tough. Real tough. You know that less than one hundred jeggies and I'm being robbed. Whad'ya say?"

I felt my blood boil with fury as they haggled. I felt fire in my soul, and I squeezed the greenish metal which kept me imprisoned. I squeezed harder and harder, and the metal blazed into my skin like electric fire, and steaming blood dripped onto the cobblestone until the veins were cauterized. She walked slowly towards the cage, tracing the bars with her claw as she approached my father.

The shadowflame at the centre of my soul exploded outwards until it simmered just the thinnest sliver beneath my skin, all around my body. It was as if all of my being and existence was merely a layer, the facade of a mask which only barely concealed a hulking mass of dark energy. I was the thinness. I was the just-above-a-nothingness. Don't give in.

Don't give in. Ignore the pain. Transcend. Push down. Fight back.

Awaken. Ascend.

Ascension.

Miss Efrezek lewdly tossed a handful of coins, without even bothering to count out the money, onto the floor. The coins spilled out and the merchant scrambled to pick them up as they rolled around the cobblestone. A pig-like monster assistant unlocked the gate and started yanking my father out of the cage by the chains around his feet. I heard a muted grunt as the roughly-pulled metal chain cut his skin. Tears welled from my eyes and poured down my cheeks, and my sight went blank for a moment with cosmonuclear rage.

I screamed for them to stop. I screamed, and I begged, and I pleaded. They did not listen.

For the second time, I heard a voice, the musicality of which rang like waves of gold. "O' Luminous One, do not give way to despair. You are your bow, Gandiva, and the cosmonuclear conflagration ever-burning within your soul is your unbounded quiver. Display for us your prowess, O' Raksha. Annihilate the darkness with your righteous fury which makes the cosmos shine with celestial effervescence."

I felt the mass of void inside of my chest shrivel rapidly, as it was crushed into the size of a baseball. And then it was a marble, and I squeezed further, until it was a grain of rice. Smaller still and it was a speck of sand, and I felt inside of me a beach, and I envisioned a cosmifinity of arrows obliterating each and every sandy crumb.

My vision went white again, totally blank. I heard no sound. There was absolute stillness which was then broken by the faintest imaginable 'ch', like a match being struck. Golden-orange flames radiated around me, and my feet levitated up off the ground. All of my hate, and all of my fury… and my anguish, and sorrow, I felt every bit of it overflow the cup of my soul. And all of it crashed down and washed over me like an apocalyptic flood.

I released the string. I heard a whisper-like chime before the celestial death of holy fire enveloped everything in front of me as the radiant explosion of a divine arrow cut through their dimension. Most of the monsters around me and all of the metal chains were disintegrated, but the Alvish were unburned. All in

182

that half-instant after my fingers let go, I watched with slowed-time as my fiery wrath consumed the merchant. A fraction of a second to him, but a gratifying half-minute for me, or so it felt.

The lady who wished to purchase my father succeeded in defending herself with a gnarled wall of green and black ice, for a moment. The light-emanating arrow burned against her icy shield, and then bore through and accelerated, and she was obliterated. Most of her was evaporated, but some of her flesh, her arms and her head, exploded away from her lack of a corpse. The Demoness' silver blood splashed against the ground and walls around her. What little remained of her after the blast dissipated into nothingness as the insuppressible fire disintegrated her remnants.

Another woman, this one with silver hair and black and purple armour, was watching from a corner atop a store roof. She successfully defended herself as she dodged out of the way. She wasn't in the direct path of my shot, nor did she seem directly involved in this aborted transaction, but she too almost perished. Each beat of my heart made a flood of energy pulse through my body and made the glittering fire which traced the outline of my aura surge chaotically.

The occasional bolt shot out, like a solar flare, and vaporized some of the monsters struggling with severe injuries, and dazed minds. By the time I turned to face my father, all of our energies were reverberating. All of the energized spirits of the Alvish, and myself, went to one realm or another. I called out to Dad, and I dropped the Gandiva, my golden bow of diamonds and rubies, but he was already gone. The divine weapon dematerialized into glowing energy which flowed back into my body. My dissolution between universes had almost finished resolving.

The last thing I heard before my eyes closed was Alianii

cheerily saying, "I really quite like your bow. It shall be mine one night!"

But I ignored her. My thoughts, and my anguish, and my golden-fire tears, rested only on my father. My father who had refused to let me perish, at the expense of one hundred and thirty-seven magi. I didn't get to ask him why. I didn't get to say goodbye.

Chapter 25

The Candent Massacre

Modern Magi History, Chapter 43, Section 5: The Candent Massacre

On 14 September, 2010, one hundred and thirty-seven magi perished in the Candent Massacre when a Voidlord self-detonated at the yearly Wing Council Commencement. Many hundreds more were severely injured. Most of the Arcane Guard Confluences in North America were immediately dispatched to investigate and protect the city in anticipation of additional attacks, although no others occurred. The circumstances of the attack became known shortly thereafter alongside the resignation, confession, and arrest of then Magister of Defense, Sebastian Candent. In his testimony, Candent informed the Arcane Guard that Da'raakan's forces had kidnapped his seven-year-old daughter, Aylene, who had been admitted to a hospital after a confirmed poisoning. In exchange for his daughter being returned without further harm, Sebastian Candent knowingly provided the access codes to enter Lunaris, which Da'raakan's forces then exploited.

The presumed targets of the void bomb were Wing Council members, alongside other high-ranking officials of the United Magisterium, and Arcane Guard officers. The majority of casualties were spouses, children and other non-combat family members in attendance. Osmidius Racond, then Grand Magister and husband of Estella Racond, who perished in the blast, officiated over the Wing Council's pronouncement, and later resigned. In accordance with the Oath of Light and a guilty plea, Sebastian Candent was executed at sunset on 15 September, the very next day. The Candent family, the patriarch of whom had originally participated in the Siege of Lunaris in 1586, was stripped of their royalty and banished from the city. Maria Candent, spouse of Sebastian and mother to Aylene, voluntarily donated all of the family's considerable wealth as reparations for the victims of the blast.

In Memory Of
Abott, Vanessa, 9 years of age
Adams, Patricia, 32 years of age
Adams, Lily, 7 years of age
Aj'anari, Kumar, 17 years of age
Apollonia, Stella, 63 years of age
Bengali, Amar, 48 years of age
Bocelli, Maria, 27 years of age
Bordeaux, Antoinette, 82 years of age
…

Chapter 26

Rage and a Twin Star Sunset

Overcome with rage and sorrow, bursting with fury and anguish, I materialized and held myself on my hands. I vomited a blend of golden blood and fire. The blood that pooled onto the stone floor had ignited and dissipated as it rapidly burned, until I added more to the pool. My head felt as if someone had picked me up by my legs and smashed me against a wall. My eyes were squinting in the futile attempt to filter out the overwhelming, piercing light of my arms and body which glowed with a supernatural fluorescence.

The rhythm of my now-returned heartbeat was closer to a machine gun than anything human. I focused on that sensation and my heartbeat accelerated even further until it was one continuous, indistinguishable stream. It was like a jet of water crashing through my soul. Everything around me felt as if it was shaking, but it was only my lack of inner stillness. I didn't realize my nakedness, which was obscured by radiating light, until the Grand Magister wrapped his coat around me as the light finally started dimming.

Walking Blizzard knelt down and helped me rise and steady myself. The vomiting had stopped. I could feel that my eyes were glazed over, and my cheeks were wet with pouring tears which turned to steam as they traced down my face. If they said anything, I couldn't hear it past the sensory overload. I closed my eyes and breathed in. I tried to eliminate one chaos at a time. I held my breath. Hold it. Hold it. Exhale. I breathed out. I breathed in again more slowly, and forced the air out again more sharply.

A pleasing coolness held my cheeks as W.B's hands gently grasped me; I can only imagine that the contrast between my still-burning self, and her frost, was painful for her. If it was, she ignored it, and I felt more of her calming frostiness flow over me as my heartbeat started to slow down. Soon I was back to a cardio-and-caffeine Aylene, as opposed to a mini-gun on amphetamines. Neither of the two bothered to ask me if I was okay, because I obviously wasn't. You probably would not benefit from asking someone if they're okay after they're impaled with a javelin, or if they're vomiting fire.

We were back in the room with all of the Somnumes and Umbrumes, although I had accidentally disintegrated about a third of them, tables included. Some of the enchanted and cursed books were still burning, and Harold, seeing his magic ineffective at dispersing the flames, allowed them to burn. I started recognizing the sounds that I realized were voices which were previously distorted, lost in that all-encompassing cacophony.

"What's wrong with me?" I managed to ask, before vomiting more golden fire, though I succeeded in turning away from W.B so as to not burn her.

It was a pointless question, because we all knew that none of us knew. The scene of my father being sold was seared into my mind, heart and soul. It was on repeat, but the playback speed was set to a thousand. I had to force myself to shift my focus away from that rage. In starting to process what I had experienced, I realized I had felt W.B's and Harold's presence

188

with me the entire time. They somehow saw, heard, smelt, felt, bled and burned everything as though they themselves were me through that surreal nightmare.

Arcane Guards warped into the room; they had sensed W.B's and Harold's aura within the military complex and located us within minutes. Harold sent them to bring me my clothing, and a female guard came back a minute later with a conjured box, inside of which she had carefully placed my formality-assessing *Of Clouds* dress and a set of undergarments. My dress, with whom my possession had created a psychic bond of sorts, had assumed the shape of typical battle raiment. I walked to the bathroom to get dressed, and the Grand Magister, W.B, and a total of four guards waited in the hallway outside.

I washed my face and mouth, and conjured a toothbrush, toothpaste and a hair brush. My attempt to tame the chaos of my hair was futile, and the redness was far more vibrant than usual.

My eyes glowed scarlet with flecks of gold and ignited fire, but if I calmed myself with a held breath for a half moment, I could bring them back to a less startling red. This effort to calm myself was somewhat lessened in net effect by the honesty by which my enchanted raiment portrayed my inner world. The moment I put them on they transformed with a conflagration vigour. In lieu of bronze armour, or the cerulean blue with periodic clouds, or even thunderstorms with rapidly crackling lightning, my garment was coloured with the furious sunburst of an all-enveloping sun. Overlaid onto that, additional blazing comet-like masses of burning matter appeared and smashed into each other in a perpetual chain of candescent explosions.

I walked outside and looked at the group awkwardly. Margarette had joined them. I stood still, and Harold raised a finger and traced it through the air over my head. He spoke in magicrypted words, but I knew what he was talking about. It was obviously the letters in Alvish script which flittered there, unseeable by me. Only W.B and Harold could see them, as well as Marvin, but he wasn't there. They no longer even needed physical contact for them to perceive the hidden symbols. The universe had branded me as a daughter of fire. I'm sure Tobias would have been pleased to see the embodied inscription.

They escorted me to the cafeteria, and I sat down, defeated, beside myself with grief, on a metal bench. It was suggested that I get myself something to eat, but the very notion of food absolutely repulsed me. W.B assembled for me a platter with a variety of things, no vegetables. She specifically got the rare-seared venison which she suspected would calm me. I tried to ignore everyone who stood around me, watching me, and I failed at doing so. I pushed the tray away, averting all of the gazes, and then Harold sat down in front of me. He had food of his own and was hungry, and I suspect he felt that him eating would encourage me to do so.

The very sound of him cutting into his food with his fork and knife grated against my mind like rusted nails against a chalkboard. I tuned out the sound, but found myself again unable to drown out the burning anguish. W.B sat down next to me and tried to coax me to eat. This ended up upsetting me further, despite her best intentions. I wasn't hungry; and yet I felt this snarling ferociousness. I felt as if I wanted my fingers to stretch out into plasma claws and rip open a hole in the fabric of reality. Breathe.

I snapped and slammed my clenched fists against the metal table, which disintegrated instantly, leaving only smouldering ash. The Grand Magister's tray fell straight down but he levitated it up so as to not splash us with sauce and the meat grease. He pushed it aside and away from us, resting it on another table. A few of the Arcane Guards shifted to a defensive battle position, but Harold lifted a hand and ordered them at ease. I was standing, only barely controlling my breath, and my fury.

"I want to leave. I want to go to Lunaris."

"Aylene…" said Harold, gently, trying to soothe me, "I think that perhaps now would not the best time for that. I am not quite sure that would be a safe or wise decision. Why don't we wait on that until you are feeling calmer; might I suggest a bath, or a video game? Why don't I call Herbert and have him come visit you here?"

"I don't want to see Herbert right now. I want to go home." The rage and anguish was getting worse.

"What about your mother or aunt?" suggested W.B. "I can only imagine how worried they are. I know it has been a while since they've… been around us all. The Grand Magister could arrange this."

Harold nodded. He and W.B were the only two who had maintained an air of calmness. The Arcane Guards were looking at me, and each other, as if I were the very manner of Demon they were accustomed to slaying. I was clearly a threat, even if unintentionally, because of my instability. Margarette Hardbub in particular looked extremely anxious. She averted the fire of my gaze as I turned to her. I looked away myself. I went back to looking at the floor, and I noticed the bareness of my feet against the smooth, magically-impervious surface.

I asked one last time, my words just above a whisper. "Please. You don't understand. I need to go home."

The Grand Magister, who now looked very sad, frowned slightly and shook his head as he denied my request. I felt the almost imperceivable tug of six out of the seven individuals around me (Margarette excluded) as they tried to lock me in place with rings of mana. I felt bands constricted ever-so-slightly around my arms, and my legs, and my ankles. Their combined force was equivalent to tens of thousands of pounds, though I wouldn't feel the resistance of weight, nor discomfort... unless I tried to move.

I felt the golden fire start to radiate just around the outline of my body, but I kept the flames from bursting outwards. I clenched my hands so hard that they were shaking, and glowing claws pierced the palms of my hand. Steaming blood dripped onto the floor. I struggled against the cuffs of mana, and they stopped me, for a moment. I pushed forward and made my way away from the group. The Arcane Guards warped back a few feet. They coalesced a synchronized dome-shaped barrier of energy around me. They thought that would stop me.

But they were wrong.

I couldn't control the fire anymore, but they were far enough away to be protected behind the defense of the barrier. My eyes went solid white, and my vision went blank. For a fraction of a nothingness of a moment, my world went back to that absolute silence.

I screamed at the top of my lungs, my voice amplified by the cosmonuclear fire which had erupted within my soul. "I WANT TO GO HOME!"

As I spoke, the bands of mana cuffing me, and the conjured barrier, shattered like millions of shards of tiny glass which instantly evaporated as they burst outwards. My golden fire enveloped me, and I warped out of the military research centre with the ease and carelessness of a cat knocking down a glass of water. I was energized, and my reverberation was faster than ever before. My oscillation was so rapid that the humming sound was deafening.

And then it stopped, and I was home; I was on the balcony of my former bedroom which overlooked most of the sacred city of my early childhood.

All at once the peace of wind surrounded me, and all of my rage was gone. I was home.

Gripping the glass rail, I looked down and saw the families, the mothers and fathers, the grandparents with their pipes indulging in huff puffery. The little tykes were running around, to-and-fro, chasing the Balloon Lizards which floated just out of their reach. I saw a neon-pink Invisiphant dash towards a fountain and suck up water with its trunk. It targeted one Balloon Lizard and shot it with a feisty jet of water. Both creatures, and the children with whom they were playing, were basking in the joy of childhood delight as the parents laughed, smiled and watched. The Invisiphant pulled in more water and climbed onto the fountain's rim which was wide enough for people to sit on. It stood on its hind legs, barely able to balance itself, and it lifted its trunk straight up and tooted repeatedly as it filled the air with fine mist.

I smiled, though my balcony was way too high up for anyone to notice me. They didn't even know I was there; and that was fine. I didn't need to be seen, I just wanted to see. I just wanted to watch. I just wanted to feel the warmth of the double Lunaris sunset as the dimming rays of the Twin Stars trailed down in invitation of spectral darkness. I could see my dress, which was in the form of battle raiment, had simmered from wrathful sun, to the tranquillity of unabated blue transitioning to a twilight unblemished.

I walked away from the edge. I quickly realized from the lack of furniture and dust-covered walls that the summer town home we lived in was completely empty. No family portraits, no

193

fridge, no oven, nothing. Not a thing; no one wanted to live here. It was a forever-vacancy, an ignored relic from a long-banished, dishonoured family. It was a somewhere else which belonged to no-one else, not even to the Candents.

Skipping the locked door and the stairs, I made myself translucent and warped down towards a corner on the city's ground. I was careful in my casting so as to not be detected. I wasn't hiding per se, but I also didn't particularly feel like broadcasting my presence. I didn't know where to go. I didn't have any Scriggets on me, nor my cell phone, and I had just defied the Grand Magister's order.

Arcane Guards were probably already looking for me, I realized, thinking, "Oh, fuck" as I looked around.

I felt someone's manascan lock on me as they tracked my aura and warped towards me. I was chased across warps. I didn't want to disturb the peace, so I went to the business district which was basically empty at that hour. Three Arcane Guards faced me a second after I finished resolving. From the shoulders down they were identical, wearing their military-grade uniform: raiment of grey, red and gold, and black Wyvernsilk Boots.

"Aylene, the Grand Magister has instructed us to provide you an escort back to your station. He wishes for me to inform you that Herbert and Marvin are on their way to Lunaris, and are expecting to see you shortly."

They had all pre-casted barriers in both hands, so they were clearly on their guard. I noticed their battle stance but didn't assume one of my own. I just stood and faced them.

"I'm not going anywhere. I'm not bothering anyone. Please leave me alone. I just need space, and I don't want to go back to the research station right now."

One of the guards tapped his wrist and made a call through the headset on his helmet, informing the recipient of our location, and what I said. Osmidius Racond, former Grand Magister and grandfather of Tobias, warped into view next to the other guards. The guards were very tense, but he ordered them at ease, and they lowered their hands. He was tall and slender with fair skin, and long white hair. He had the same dark eyes as Tobias. His hair was fastened with a traditional male braid for the holiday season, and he was wearing casual raiment, not armour. Osmidius conjured a table and chairs for us and asked that I sit down with him. I sat down, saying nothing. I felt more apathetic and resigned than nervous, though I averted the intensity of his gaze.

"Aylene, I do not find your countenance threatening. I'm not quite caught up on all of the details just yet but Harold requested that I check on you."

"You must hate me," I said plainly, which I did suppose at the time to be true, considering his wife, Tobias' grandmother, had perished in the void bomb when I was a little girl.

"Do not so hastily characterize my relationship with grief," he said. "I have had warring sons, child. Dragons are as prone to clashing as they are to greatness. I am here, as I have stated, to check on you as per my old friend's request. I mean you no harm, though I do wish to ask you something."

"Ask away, sir," I said to the former leader of our country.

"Our city has been in significant turmoil on account of the incident with you, Tobias and Marvin. I have read a report which characterizes your account as provided to the Grand Magister, alongside a couple of Marvin's recent contributions."

"The Umbrume... yeah. What a fuck up. What about it?"

"When the three of you encountered a Noc'raakan, the entity instructed all three of you to choose someone to sacrifice," said Osmidius, "and it tortured you in a period of, and I quote from the report, 'timelessness' until such a point that the first person selected another. Is that correct?"

195

"It was my fault for not sacrificing myself. Tobias didn't want to offer Marvin."

"As a matter of fact, I have a suspicion that he didn't," said Osmidius, as he put one finger on his lips in thinking. "It would be a curious thing otherwise then that all three of you survived. Marvin's account, as he has recalled more of the event since his recovery, notably differs from your own."

The Grand Magister and a few other Arcane Guards materialized, and the other guards paralleled the at-ease. Osmidius and Harold spoke for a few minutes in magicrypted words, though I don't think I would have bothered listening anyway. No one would get it if they hadn't been there themselves; even what Harold and W.B saw was nothing next to what Marvin and Tobias went through.

They had been tortured by a deity for an infinity minus one times infinity. Harold asked me if I felt calm, and I answered that I did. Numb, in truth, was a more perfect answer. I wasn't fatigued, but I felt emotionally stunted. It was like I took all of the wrath I felt and put it in a glass box on a shelf in my closet, though I also could feel that I could open it, if I so wanted. Or if someone pushed me.

"I am confident that Miss Candent is not a threat," concluded Osmidius. "And who better than myself to understand an incendiary spirit? Harold, let her rest at your winter cottage and have Herbert and Marvin meet her in a few hours. That is my counsel, old friend."

The current Grand Magister listened to Osmidius thoughtfully, and slowly approached me, holding his hands together in a gesture of serenity. "Would such a prospect be in accordance with your wishes? Herbert and Marvin are both quite eager to see you; it is a most exquisitely-cosy manner of lodging, I can assure you, and its offerings well-stocked. Now, I know you're not hungry. You have effectively conveyed the vigorousness of your sentiments; but I would hardly be a Hardbub if I didn't allude to my epicurean entourage."

I agreed, and Harold Hardbub dismissed the other guards and escorted me to a warp station at the main plaza. He tapped a sequence of fifteen out of the more than one hundred glyphs on the control panel. The two of us warped and appeared at the centre of a village. There were maybe forty or so smallish homes within sight, a couple stores, and all of the buildings were traditional magi forest cabins. Bright stripes, primarily pastels, colours which harmonized with the softened winter. I saw a group of senior citizens, veterans in their retirement coats adorned with their badges. They stood on a porch with a few pipes and I could smell the Choconut Sunrises in the mugs they were holding.

Four children, dressed warmly, were dancing with a beat-boxing Enlivened Snowman with a bowtie and sunglasses. Small Pyrinines of non-burning flame were playing with young Ice Deer. Their mirth was watched by the Crystalhorn Stags which relaxed at the top of a small hill. Where the laypeople have streetlights or lamp posts, we had floating lengths of ropes adorned with many aged-bronze lanterns which swayed slightly in the wind and illuminated the town. Harold and I walked through a short forest path and stopped at their family cabin. The home combined the traditional architecture of the village with an opening into a den built into a hollowed-out hill. The Grand Magister gave me a quick tour. He showed me the bedrooms and the stunningly-stocked kitchen, and the bathrooms and closets with a variety of extra clothing. Perks of being a guest at this Hardbub clan cottage include family-crested bathrobes made from Cave Cotton, and an abundant variety of truffle breads.

Chapter 27

Born of Sky and Snow

After freshening up, I used the house phone and called my aunt Susan, who lived with her husband Mike in a coastal town near Boston. She was happy to hear from me. I told her that I'd been seriously injured in a training accident at school, and I apologized for not contacting her or Mother sooner. Mom was visiting family up in the Kandenthakan Mountains. Those mountain villages are one of the few places where you find more traditional magi who don't use any electronics, unless they are in a modern city. They prefer Animaletters, enchanted wooden-based slabs which transformed into small, wooden sculpture projections as they played a story or delivered a message. They took months to make, and were expensive if you went out and bought and configured one. Getting one is a big deal. Depending on the privacy level (marked in a symbol on the side of the wood), when the villagers get one, they go out to the plaza and invite others to watch.

I asked about my mom Maria, who was both saddened of heart and stoic; she wore her suffering in silence, and asked for pity from no one. My mother and aunt both acted with the dignity of former noblewomen, with kindness and demeanours characterized by warmth. Mom was no doubt finding a mellow joy in her visit. Although I wanted to see her, I was relieved that the Grand Magister didn't send for her. It could take up to a week traverse through that winding desert valley, and it was almost unthinkable to warp out unless it was a catastrophic emergency. Tradition would have meant having to spend another week on the trail just to get back.

I looked around the Hardbub den and noticed the presence-detecting fireplace which filled the air with hints of cherry wood. A spice roaster had turned itself on and set itself to aromatic mode as it crushed magi freshened cacao beans, cloves of cinnamon, and began pre-heating. I sat on a sofa chair in the den which faced some of the frosted-glass windows through which I saw the fuzzied lights of our floating winter lanterns. Harold had called the home earlier and told me that Herbert and Marvin would come over once they finished dinner in Lunaris.

It felt like an eternity (a layperson "eternity". I'm somewhat exaggerating; it wasn't cosmic torture or anything), until I saw the two Hardbubs coming up the path. They waved at me and walked over. Herbert stopped for a moment and examined some of his berry bushes before he entered. He's almost, but not quite, one-track-minded. For plants. He had been trying to get me to learn about the spice trade which he worked on in the logistics lab, but I was terribly uninterested.

I met Marvin at the door and gave my friend a hug. I had only known Marvin for about four months, but I had sailed with him on Alvish wing ships. We had toured a few parts of an encapsulated South Pacific on a Darmish zeppelin. The two of us had explored the mysterious and mostly-empty ruins of Darmish cities, which were characterized by all sorts of bizarre metal machines which repeated their actions unceasingly. We'd stumbled upon a Golem, the fate of which was the nearly perpetual sweeping of slowly accumulated imaginary dust. It is remarkable how a few layperson hours can become days or weeks through a Somnume or Umbrume. The two of us had shared magic dreams, and we had mutually endured cosmic nightmares.

"We've all been worried about you, ya know," said Marvin, who was wearing a peacoat over one of his signature over-sized forest green hoodies and a blue starpuff beanie.

He took off his coat and boots and started preparing the magi equivalent of magically-enhanced hot cocoas for the three of us. He briefly held up a deck of cards for a quick moment with an eager grin. I still had a debt of Glyphwalkers to pay off; though the Hardbubs (once bankers) did not charge interest. Herbert walked inside. I was still at the door, and I gave him a longer hug, and he kissed me on the lips.

"Hi, Herbie," I said, as Herbert shed some of his winter layers.

He gave me a funny scrunching of the face. He tolerated it when I called him as such, so long as I didn't do in front of his Lambda Tau brothers. His buddy Martin (of the Von Bears, one of the other Great Houses) teased him a little too much when I first did that. Herb was wearing a wintergreen dress shirt, the shade of which cycled through a subtle range of similar shades. His candy-cane bowtie was a pattern of continually swirling white and red. Magi fashion may strike you as a little eccentric, but we are a fond-of-visual-spectacle people. Our three-dimensional fireworks and art incantations set a high standard for what is chic, and what is boring.

Marvin handed each of us a Choconut Sunrise, which is a hot cocoa with coconut oil for a silky texture with high-grade Ceylon cinnamon, whipped cream and Pyrinine Milk. Magi often enjoy this energizing drink during winter in advance of games, adventures and just-as-frequent mischief and tomfoolery. Within reason, we were granted the month of December to prank our families and community members.

One of our traditions had for hundreds of years involved attempting to sneak Dragon Pepper Dust into the cinnamon jar of any person who had red smoke coming from their chimney. The Magistorians believe this was the modern reinvention of various forms of survival preparation games of childhood that the magi needed for millennia. Demons used to hunt us brazenly, until we eradicated most of them. Now we just had to deal with the rifts and the Demons that came through them.

The signifying red smoke indicated participation, and it came from the wood of the mountain cherry and filled the outside air with a sweet fruitiness. If you got caught, you had to eat a full pepper of whatever size that particular magi happened to have in their spice room (in accordance with their mercy or lack thereof). As for the spice keeper, you can't just let perfectly-good emblazoned Ceylon cinnamon go to waste.

We also had snowball traps. If you're careful you can detect the shift in the manafield surrounding a surreptitiously snow-covered glyph. If you didn't see it, you were the impromptu recipient of a simultaneous barrage of anywhere from two to forty-two or more snowballs. And that trap was open game for everybody; no one was exempt. Not even the veterans, who, if anything, enjoyed the joy of childhood magi more than anyone. It meant that their sacrifices had succeeded enough for them to be there, in that moment, in the magic that is the company of little loved ones.

Herbert, Marvin and I caught up as we sat at a table in the den and played Glyphwalkers together. I told them about most aspects of my experiences with the Umbrume and Cosmoria.

201

Marvin's eyes opened wide when I told him about the hurricane, Hydroxis, the "Emperor of Storm" who his uncle had mind broken. It is difficult to defeat a Voidlord, and it is unheard of to do so without actually killing or severely harming it. I told them about that Cosmorian world I sort of visited... it was weird... it was like I was Alianii, but I also wasn't.

Herbert joked when I told him about the mushroom creature, calling it a waste that it wasn't roasted first and topped with honey brie. Marvin gave him a funny look, and I brushed it aside and told them about the hunting. Then I explained Papano and his band of dancing-and-instrument-playing skeletons from beasts and monsters with the Ribrattle Xylophones and Nightforged Trumpets. I skipped the murdered pumpkin, and I glossed over most of the details of when the Alvish and I were slaves.

"Umm... it wasn't very pleasant. There were Alvish in cages and they were being sold as slaves. I managed to break out of the cage and I stopped them with an energy attack. Then I woke up at the research station."

Marvin was enthralled. He was almost shivering with excitement as we played and talked. He asked me, "What kind of energy attack? Did you cast a spell? What were the activating words? What did it look like?"

"Err... a golden bow sort of appeared in my hands," I explained sheepishly. "I just kind of shot it, didn't say any words or anything. I mean I heard a sort of chime sound. It... destroyed a few of the monsters, and the Demon Queen, who was trying to buy someone."

Herbert could tell that I was a little uncomfortable or upset, and he switched the topic to what was going on with school and the upcoming Yesteryear Ball. He took incompletes on two courses but had finished the work for the others, and just had one final project and an exam to take by the end of January. Marvin explained that he had pretty much fully recovered, and that he was considering starting school up again in the spring semester, or a research project. If either of my two Hardbubs was upset with me, their faces didn't show it, though I had a feeling that Herbert was still uneasy about everything.

It was a few pleasant hours later when the wind picked up, and I heard the sound of bits of snow hitting the side of the cabin. We were just kind of relaxing. Herbert was casually pruning some of his winter plants in the garden behind the house (who does that at night, like seriously)? Marvin and I had finally taken a break from playing, and he was sitting in one of his corners, reading one of his textbooks. I was watching the wintery forest through the window, reflecting on my circumstances. The thought of the personalitied textbook Fábulito popped into my head; he would've liked this log cabin. As long as I didn't sit too close to the fireplace, of course. He was probably still in my bedroom on campus.

The snowstorm picked up until the sky-obscuring flurries of white were so thick you basically couldn't see anything. I could barely perceive the evergreens donning their arctic coats, and the skies of winter grey were made less bleak by the glowing white of snow-blanketed earth. Herbert came in to take a shower, and Marvin and I were surprised when, not ten minutes later, we heard a quick succession of small thud sounds and squeaking. We walked over to the front door and opened it. I was quite surprised, and slightly annoyed, to find that there were two Crystal Constructs which had been stationed outside of the lodging.

The glowing blue of their eyes on their rapidly rotating spherical heads immediately met our gaze as they turned to greet us. As if to complain, both lifted their floating stone arms outwards and pointed at a whiskered, child-sized creature. It was standing and watching us, from next to a tree not ten feet away, throwing crudely-made snowballs at the door to get our attention. It was a Kobold Scout. I could tell right away because of the long and wrinkly brown skin of the rat-like snout, and the whiskers and the armour made of bark. This encounter seemed to rather upset the Crystal Constructs, who were making all sorts of odd beeps and whirs.

I gasped. "A Kobold! You guys didn't tell me there were Kobolds here. It's so cute!"

A lot of people think Kobolds are ugly; I think they're adorable. Yes, they sort of resemble a walking rat, but they are sweet, and endearingly mischievous. As a matter of fact, the Spirits of the forest have a symbiotic relationship with us. We protect them and they plant and maintain an abundance of forest fruits, vegetables and various spices and herbs. They have a hard time understanding money, but they do understand hand-gestured trading.

The creature's eyes were glowing like a raccoon at night, and it brought its tiny, wrinkly-skin clawed hand to its mouth. It whistled. A shrill whistle of a loudness that I have not heard in a whistle, certainly not from a creature of that size and appearance. Imagine our surprise when a little troop of perhaps twenty-five or thirty kobolds appeared with remarkable haste. Some jumped down from hidden spots in the trees, as if the whole time they had been hugging the trunks in their stealthy reconnaissance. Just as many sprinted over from further in the forest. It is perhaps worth noting that Kobolds, on account of their clumsiness, do not sprint particularly quickly. They did, however, exert a great and visible effort in their attempts at expediency, as they fell over one another dashing through snow.

Except for the cabin behind us, we were surrounded by the whiskered, tailed creatures. Some were hopping from foot to foot, wiggling their hands in the air. A haphazard, misguided attempt at looking menacing. Others did the dancing, jumping sort of thing, too. But instead of the finger wiggles, they tried to intimidate us by pulling and twirling their whiskers. A subgroup looked rather determined and had formed an assembly line of sorts. Three were forming snowballs, two were digging a box-like nook, and two were shuttling back and forth to ferry their ammunition from their aforementioned allies to their makeshift fortress.

One of the Crystal Constructs, seeing the dastardly intent of these baffling little beings, resolved itself to take decisive action. It stomped its stone slab feet into the snow. It compacted the snow into crunchy ice, and then the Construct charged forward at a Kobold. The selection of the particular Kobold was either random or unclear, like a dice-roll rhinoceros. In but half of a second, the Construct had sprung forward, instantly grabbing the Kobold with spontaneously generated mana fingers which glowed like the Northern Lights.

The Construct then spun around in a rapid swirl - mostly for show, I suspect - and then leaned back. It catapulted the unfortunate, rather surprised-looking Kobold through the blizzarding sky. In a perfect arc it flew back; thank goodness we answered the door. I managed to managrasp him. Had I not done so, the little fellow would have experienced a most perilous collision; he wouldn't have coalesced until the beginning of *next* winter. I scolded the Constructs which beeped at me, apparently upset with my intervening.

I carefully levitated the Kobold down to the ground and it

scurried over behind some of its friends where it shivered with fright. Poor thing. The Kobolds looked at each other, utterly shocked. One of the larger, older and important-looking Earth Spirits made a squeaking sound which called them together for an important discussion. Seeing his opportunity, Marvin told me to stay there, and ran into the house before emerging just a minute later. He was now holding a large sack with a rough texture which resembled the pine leaf and bark outfits that some of the Kobolds were wearing.

One of the many Hardbub hustles is the generous exchange with, and sometimes free gifts to, these rather capricious and fussy creatures. Herbert's great grandfather had discovered a particular troop of Kobolds in Africa that refused to trade any of their scavengeables for anything but onions from Walla Walla. The same offering to an Everglades entourage was received so angrily that it resulted in the Apple Snail Feud of 1894. It's because of *us* that Miami is nicknamed the Magic City, by the way.

Slowly, carefully, with one hand lifted up to indicate peaceful intentions, Marvin approached the troop of Kobolds who had turned to watch him. The Elder and a few of the larger (still child-sized) Kobolds were quite clearly upset with the Constructs. Some were nudging each other, excited or frantic, and a few resumed pulling their whiskers. Marvin identified for me the Elder among them (every Kobold troop has between one and three Elders). You can tell them apart through the white hair and double-pronged curly moustaches. Even the female Elders have these, though their skin is more orange-ish than brown, and they have longer hair. Marvin was holding a sack with light-blue mushrooms with white splotches; Glacial Mushrooms. All of the Kobolds, and I do mean all of them, were sent into a frenzy of absolute exuberance.

They hopped around, only going up each hop the barely three or four inches they could manage, grabbing each other with glee. After a minute of this commotion, the Elder gestured for them to settle down, and bowed. He walked forward and put his hands out, and Marvin gave him the bag. The troop leader stroked his moustache politely, and bowed once more, holding the bow respectfully before turning around. A loud but less obnoxious whistle was the command, and the troop of Kobolds turned about face. They marched away and back into the evergreen forest adorned by winter's white.

Before they left, the Kobold I saved scurried over to me and hugged my leg. It bent over and kissed the exposed skin on the top of my cosy, slippered foot. It then bowed before me three times, and ran back to catch up with the others. It may surprise you to know that I did, on a much later day, come to know more of the fate of that far-flung Kobold. The tale of the tailed and whiskered fellow who went up as no other Kobold ever had.

To the best of my knowledge, that is, as Constructs and Kobolds do not happen upon each other on frequent occasion. The little legend of the Earth Spirit who had ascended, who achieved apotheosis, transmuted by the arctic wind. He was airborne like the Icarus of ancient myth, but was saved by serendipity. Its wings were not fated to melt in the blazing sun. The whiskered one would crunch many more Glacial Mushrooms. It would gulp more cherry wood stew; a light-hearted tale for a one-day reprieve from darkness.

Chapter 28

A Yesteryear Rescinded

It is on the 31 December that magi around the world celebrate Yesteryear. It is an appreciation of life for those who lived, and it is a remembrance of lost loved ones. The entire month is the joy of intermittent surprises of small gifts and winter sweets, but all of it culminates on that final evening before January. The evening where our festivities commemorate the lore of our innate gifts by which our lives are defined. Magic said to be blessed upon us by the Travelers, two halves of the same one God, the merciful Mother of luck and prosperity, and her consort, Father Justice. Our gifts, we generally believe, are imparted unto us, "that we may suppress the darkness of their shadow." Some among us believe that it was the Seraphim to whom magic was first granted, and from them descended the Alvish, that ancient race to whom we are connected by some measure of blood. You have never seen a debate until you've seen two elixired Magistorians and a post-huffpuffery Astral Cosmologist exchange rhetoric to woo research funding from a Raj'Pathani prince.

The United Magisterium hosted our gala at the Tallening Tower, on the twenty-fourth floor. Many a mage had, over the centuries, unfortunately experienced psychosis following an attempt to ascend the entirety of the unbounded-height building. Illusions, contradictions, and paradoxes, the building defied the notions of space and time as understood by the physicists of the laypeople. The madness would increase steadily as if the effort to ascertain the truth of this mystic place was a divine offense worthy of a punishment equal to one's persistence. Eventually, inevitably, the mage in question gave up or else had their mental state deteriorate to the point that they were considered to be of an inherent danger to others and were relocated accordingly.

The first forty floors were habitable and were used as the offices for various government functions. The gala floor where the event is hosted is a wide, disk-like plaza. The enchantments from the Alvish persisted still. Thin water trails traced a labyrinth of paths around the entirety of the area and lifted upwards in defiance of gravity. Some of the translucent rooms were largely defined by the Starquartz panels which depicted narrative archetypicals. The ceiling was of a dazzling surrealness that could compete with Cosmoria, but without the embodied demonic planets which watched and waited. In lieu of carnivorous auroras, the colours wavered in shade together, in a unified harmony.

You can't see that people are up on that plaza-like floor above Lunaris; people below see only sky. But we were there, and the group of adults laughed, wined, and dined with a menagerie of elixirs and exotic exquisitries. As most will attest, the most festive, and history-worthy of Yesteryears generally (but not exclusively) occurs under an era of Hardbub. That is of course rhetorically charged, and hinges upon the general unwillingness of most magi to make their way across the Cockatrice Desert to get to Jaipurthani The members of the Great House Raj'Pathani possessed the only sky ship in the world which still functioned.

The evening was going more smoothly than my anxiety had

anticipated. I had for many days before that evening been stuck in a weird back and forth with myself, and with Herbert. I kept feeling that the event would be a catastrophe, the possibility of which Herbert would downplay as he tried to comfort me. Then I would feel more confident about the occasion. This led to the now-worried Herbert being unsure as to the nature of fireworks such an evening might entail, and what my contributions to those fireworks might be. And then I felt grief, and woe, and seven sorrows; the thought of not being able to go to the most important celebration of my people was unbearable. Then, of course, Herb would comfort me, and so I was stuck in this alternating loop of duty-and-culture chess as I flipped between giddy anticipation and absolute despair.

But there I was. I, like everyone, had ascended the twenty-four flights of stairs. My dress was a starlit night with the gradual rotation of bands of the Milky Way. Pleasant flurries of snow, not freshly falling but kissed by wind and lovingly lifted, added to the fabric's motion. It had assumed a more sensuous cut and shape which matched the elegance of the other magi men and women in attendance at the very formal, very-rowdy, occasion.

Harold in his first year as Grand Magister some time ago had coined the phrase, "It would be an unforgivable misfortune to perish on a Tuesday, when I could have *lived* on Yesteryear."

Note then that "Tuesday" is what our humanities teachers explain as being "the ambiguous Tuesday", where the actuality of Monday is the day immediately after Yesteryear. This context ignores the actual calendar (Monday to Sunday) day, for the net effect is Tuesday's becoming of "The day after the day when I anticipated my hangover ending, and participation in the work force resuming."

I had danced with Herbert for some time; our hands phase

shifted together as he led during one of the couple-oriented Yesteryear melodies. I am quite fond of that moment; Herbert was, as always, particularly dashing. He was wearing a pastel, powder-blue suit with a silver trim. His charcoal grey dress shirt had an overlay of gold and white fireworks. It was certainly festive, but the speed of the fireworks was much slower and more subtle than some of the more intense spectacles on display. After a few dances, and a quick kiss near one of the balconies, I asked to be left alone. It was all too much. I felt overwhelmed with joy and sadness. I looked out into the celestial night. I only barely suppressed tears, and my mind wandered to thoughts of Alianii and Tobias. I wondered if they were still out there, somewhere; maybe Alianii was me.

I went back to the more crowded area and my eyes happened upon the outfit of a Raj'Pathani prince. Raj'Pathani ceremonial raiment are typically encoded with loops of embroidered animations of some of their multiple-day religious festivals. If you look at one for a few seconds, the observer display pops up in your vision. You can change the speed of the show (as you alone perceive it) with the interface. You can leave it playing, close it, or walk away and skip a few colourful days while you refilled your huff puffery pipe, or added another elixir to your chalice. Raiments and dresses encoded as such can take over five years to make, and they are typically worn once, so as to be talked about forever, immortalized by once-ness.

Herbert was off somewhere socializing, probably with Martin and the Raj'Pathanis, finishing his chalice of Stormeye Rum and who-knows-what-else as they discussed a cultivational exchange. It is literally impossible to mention the name Raj'Pathani to a Hardbub without hearing them go on and on about their spices. I'd already heard the spiel like twelve times.

The Raj'Pathanis *only* sold eighty-eight of their one hundred and seventeen signature spices. That meant that the poor Hardbub in question would be unable to partake of any of the many local-only cuisines and inebriated spice states, without first traversing, without warping or using a motorized vehicle, a nearly three-hundred-mile desert. On future visits, they would have one of their captains pick you up by sky ship. I wonder why the Raj'Pathanis seldom have guests.

The evening progressed, and then it was time for the Yesteryear speech. The Grand Magister had endured the varied effects from, as Herbert proudly recalls, at least eleven different categories of elixir. That is to say, multiple drinks from each of the aforementioned eleven categories. I will not attempt to blanket the truth of the magi drinking problem. But I will emphasize the context of our Demon problem; there is really a remarkably unsettling variety of all sorts of supernatural, cosmic, unholy and arcane unpleasantries with which magi contend.

I was there, towards the front of the crowd, not out of a particular desire to be, because I do not much care for nor benefit from public attention, but because Herbert had to be. Only a small fraction of all of the people in attendance fit in the room. It was a notable Honora, but Harold's words projected through the magic walls with perfect resonance. It was as if the building itself, the water, the glass-like Starquartz, it was as if the very building had been attuned to deliver his voice. And it had; such was the magic and the mystery of the tower, ancient and unsolved.

"To the Darkness, then, I cheer," said Harold, hiccupping, with little sparks of pink sizzling electricity in his magically-whitened hair. "For by their wretched contrast, they imply the Higher Lights. And so are we the wildfire, to their parched grass."

Harold shivered, and rubbed his eyes before steadying himself as he continued speaking.

"It is with joy the depth of which is impossible to overstate that I speak to you all, on our blessed evening of Yesteryear. May *God* remind me of the humility by which I strive to lead you. It is a joy made all the more profound by our solemn remembrance of all of those who have come before us, in this year, and in the Yesteryears before them since time immemorial. Always, *always,* shall we remember their collective sacrifice. From now until the end of days, may never it come, are we compelled by Honora and grace to remember their courage. We will not mourn this year, not on this evening; we will instead revel in the glory of the history of our people, and our light. We will not sit idly by and be muffled by despair; we will roar with the light of *triumph!*

"And it is to that later point that I have an announcement to make. The Wing Council has convened and, after significant deliberation, has approved this release just in time for this merry moment. On 17 December, a group of Magicryptographers led by Erin Von Bear and funded by the United Magisterium, with a particularly generous donation by the Raj'Pathanis, successfully decoded the Alvish language. We have since verified their results and have, as of this very day, catalogued and analysed the contents of over twenty tomes. To put this in perspective, prior to 17 December, we had only understood two-hundred and twenty-eight of their words, and many of those only in a few contexts.

"The team of researchers is working to create a generalized theory based off of their experimental results, but a phrase of interest they are using is 'probabilistic language'. One sentence of twenty of their Alvish words, it was shown, can have over ten semantically valid, complex sentence equivalents. For those of us who revelled-and-rowdied through school, such as yours truly, this means that reading (or not-reading) one textbook in their language could mean reading ten in ours. Surely there is no greater darkness than the thought of that many textbooks - and an assignment thereafter."

The crowd laughed and cheered, and our Grand Magister bowed haphazardly before continuing.

"Furthermore, it has been observed that there is a significant decrease in the attacks on our Warpgates. Several rifts have closed, and many others have shrunk significantly. For the first time in nearly sixteen years, we successfully slew an Abyssal Watcher without a casualty. The Alvish books that we are analysing as we further refine our analytics methodology happen to contain rather useful infor…"

"All light is fated for dissipation to an omitted echo's fragment, be assimilated," said the voice of Dresha'kan as our realm was annihilated, as we became quark soup, as the city of Lunaris was swallowed by a Voidlord singularity. The Noc'raakan had planted a Voidlord bomb who knows how many centuries ago.

We were first electrons, protons, neutrons, all the -ions and -tons crushed underneath psuedo-infinite tonnage. It just so happened that there was a Voidlord glyph that had waited, like a cosmic nightmare mine, for a very specific set of conditions. When the primary speaker, surrounded by mostly silence, repeatedly used language that referred to decoding, reading or understanding the Alvish language, it would trigger. All of our governmental leaders, high-ranking military officials, and every prominent member of the Great Houses, the business community and most of our professors, were collectively confetti. We were just dispersed into nothingness soup and sloshed together. There aren't really better ways to describe it.

It was a serendipitous thing, then, that I was somewhat acquainted with our current predicament, and I was able to materialize.

I entered my Raksha form. The radiance of golden flames surrounded my body as I floated through void. I shifted my mind to the reality of our hosted-on-a-disc gala. I had claws like flaming knives, and I did not see with my eyes but by heat and anti-heat. I saw by pockets of dread and sorrow and soul, and by bubbles of hope. I envisioned the Voidlord in a corporeal form. I imagined it as the Demon Queen, with her ruby-red skin, and her disgusting snake eyes of yellow.

That golden-clawed red Demon bitch, I grabbed her legs and tore her in half. I smashed the two sides of her into themselves as if I was crushing together two pieces of aluminium foil. I ripped open the aluminium foil ball as if pulling her neck back into existence, so I could obliterate her with cosmic fire breathed down her throat. I ripped and split her ribs into smaller and smaller shards of bone as I improved upon Papano's skeleton ensemble. I eviscerated the Demoness into a Splinterscorch Violin with strings made from her shredded soul, and the instrument's body was made from the dust of her twice-scorched bones.

I made her drag her violin through the Cockatrice Desert, but she was doomed to be consumed as a continually-born-again mouse. Cockatrice-consumed at an inch, a mile, mile seventy-eight, mile two hundred and ninety-nine point nine nine nine. Nine. Her tears repeatedly flooded the world, and drowned her, and she was the nutrients by which plankton grew. She grew into a shrimp that I had caught by sea hustling children. I flayed her and served her in lemon juice on a many-years-ago Yesteryear, and I gave her to Harold. He thanked me, profusely.

215

The Demon Queen's cosmic torture was celestial jazz, where every infinitesimal fraction of a note, much less the intricacies of paradox chords, punished her hubris times a gold fire trillion. I trapped the Voidlord mouse in her sandy universe. I put her universe inside of a water droplet, and I was her once-in-a-Yuga drought. Her suffering was a quadrillion quadrillions. She was a world-stopping, plague-bringing virus, and I was her atmosphere of Venus punishment. My acid clouds cleaved the void carbon anti-atoms in her body. She was clay, and I was the basket of chisels which repeatedly carved her shapelessness; and the arrogant Demoness, was nevermore.

With the Voidlord's infinite death, I attained my Redemption.

Chapter 29

AC9K-2020/21 SUMMARY REPORT

Case ID: <u>AC9K-2020/21</u>

Distributed: 15 January 2021, 09:00 AM (MGI-STD), **SECRECY: ECHO+5**

Report Title (BRIEF): ENERGY CONTAINMENT RISK

Report Title (LONG): A statistical approximation of a longevity anomaly as a predictive model to explain the spirit power level as measured in Aylene Candent.

Findings Brief: Following the void bomb of Yesteryear, a formal analysis of the threat level of female, 18, Aylene Candent, was deemed necessary. This report was proposed by Osmidius Racond (Senior Wing Councilman), who informally observed her spirit power level to be between 9400 and 9500. The data in the table below is used in our current model. This exploratory approach resulted in a predictive accuracy of 98.675 percent, with the model's predicted value as OSL(Observed Spirit Level)=9514 as compared to Aylene's lab-measured OSL=9642 Aylene's OSL anomaly appears to be related to the combined predictive lifespan of the 137 magi who died in the Candent Massacre of 2010. Mathematically, the only conceived explanation for Aylene's spirit power level is that the souls of the victims, and their longevity, merged with Aylene Candent's. The exact mechanism by which this occurred is unclear and perhaps can most humbly described as miraculous. At a power level of 9642, Aylene exceeds nine ascensions or power tiers above an ordinary mage, making her more dangerous than all known laypeople nuclear weapons, were all of her spirit power to be converted to energy simultaneously.

Assumptions: Average Life Expectancy of 118

Age Range	Range Average	Victims	Long. Gap	Total Lifespan
1 - 8	4.5	8	113.50	908.00
9 - 16	12.50	6	105.50	633.00
17 - 24	20.50	19	97.50	1852.50
25 - 32	28.50	17	89.50	1521.50
33 - 40	36.50	23	81.50	1874.50
41 - 48	44.50	8	73.50	588.00
49 - 56	52.50	4	65.50	262.00
57 - 64	60.50	8	57.50	460.00
65 - 72	68.50	7	49.50	346.50
73 - 80	76.50	12	41.50	498.00
81 - 88	84.50	10	33.50	335.00
89 - 96	92.50	5	25.50	127.50
97 - 104	100.50	7	17.50	122.50
105 - 112	108.50	3	9.50	28.50
113 - 120	116.50	3	1.50	4.50
121 - 128	124.50	3	-6.50	-19.50
129 - 136	132.50	2	-14.50	-29.00

Total Victims	137	
Predicted Lifespan	9514	
Measured Lifespan	9642	
Accuracy	98.67%	

Epilogue

The moment I suspected something was up was when I looked around the Grand Magister's office and noticed that there were no foodstuffs, nor food-themed decorations. There was not even a single cooking apparatus. No posters, no sets of mini-fridges, no triple-layer globes with hidden compartments of Jadefire Cigars or auto-refilling racks of cheeses. If you ever find yourself in an important meeting with a Hardbub, and no food or drinks are offered, know then that in all probability, someone is in danger. I didn't think that to be me, nor did I detect any reason for Harold to be acting so nervously. He was humming as he rummaged through a file cabinet, apparently looking for something. The Grand Magister turned around and our eyes met. He looked as if he was a deer caught in headlights.

"Grand Magister, sir," I said. "Did you lose something? Why don't I help you fi…"

"Oh, that's not necessary. Here it is," said Harold, exasperated for some reason, bringing in an envelope which he placed gingerly on the desk as he sat down. He tapped it a few times, then held his finger down on the paper sleeve. Harold was going to slide it over to me, but he had something to say first.

"Now, I don't usually have meetings during ice storms, nor on Tuesdays, and certainly not on such days of intersection," said Harold. "But alas, here we are. My only regret is not indulging in a third Choconut Sunrise. May the Mother's dice roll in our favour."

The Grand Magister lifted his finger and allowed me to open the envelope, and look through the papers inside. There was a summary report with my "observed spirit level" which, apparently, approached ten thousand. I glanced at a table filled with numbers, and these added up to... one hundred and thirty-seven. Oh. *Oh.* I glanced around a bit more, but I felt an uneasiness which was quickly giving way to sorrow. I put the papers away and closed the envelope.

"The term the Sages have decided upon is 'Post-Void Hypermana Disorder'. Normally I would say ask your Sage if you have any questions, but *you* are the question, my dear."

Harold and I looked at each other, and there was a quiet moment. It was not uncomfortable; it was just a sort of knowing pause.

"After extensive and difficult deliberation, we made the decision to disclose that information to you, Miss Candent. I am sorry if what you have read troubles you."

"I'm not sure I see the wisdom in informing me as to why I'm considered a threat," I said. "Just banish me from the city, then."

Harold paused for a moment, carefully contemplating his words before he spoke.

"We cannot, nor do we wish to. I will re-emphasize that this decision was made after a lengthy council meeting with various proponents taking no less than six distinct positions. Ultimately, we settled upon this... forthrightness. It is wiser, we hope, for you to know your power, so that you act with caution, than for you to live in the destructive shadow of ignorance. No, Aylene, we would not risk banishing you, if from love and fear in equal, hefty-even-for-a-Hardbub, portions. Your actions and aspect on Yesteryear, where you were terror incarnate, saved all of our people."

"Then I don't understand what the problem is, if I'm seen as a hero."

"I am not fond of the word 'problem' in this context - well, maybe predicament is a better term. But that's the same thing... oh. Well, on a related note, Aylene, I also wish to congratulate you and inform you of your official promotion to Voidslayer of the Arcane Guard. Alongside this, in the interest of maximizing the probability of safety, you have been approved to be decommissioned and begin an early, joyous retirement."

"Excuse me?"

"Your pension has been set to 184,000 Scriggets annually, adjusted for inflation, paid biweekly, and you shall receive a travel allow-"

"WHAT!" I blurted out, my palms slapping the desk a little forcefully, but without incinerating it. "I'm promoted to *Voidslayer* and you're making me retire. What a lengthy, award-ridden and fulfilling career! Please tell me you're joking."

Harold shook his head, his hands were trembling, and I lifted my hands in sarcastic joy. "If *only* my classmates from back in the day were still alive, so I could thank them. I'm EIGHTEEN. Retired. *Retired.* Kicked out of the military before I even graduated school, more like it. Is that an order? Can I appeal this decision?"

"We considered it likely that you might ask about this. For now, the answer is no, but who is to say that we cannot revisit the topic again someday? You certainly have unique abilities, and ferocities," said Harold, "but wise are the gaily grass men who do not nonchalantly dance with cosmic wildfire. I'll have you know that there are many soldiers, and ordinary citizens, who have panic attacks upon the very sight of you. Reflect upon that for some time, my child. It is with infinite gratitude, joy, and a carefully-measured truffle spoon of empathized sorrow, that we thank you. We humbly recognize that we can never truly know your burden. Do not ask us for labour, or combat, Aylene. Do not act in need of redemption. We are not so ungracious so as to add one more moment of burden to our newfound Saint of Righteous Fury."

My Grand Magister gestured for me to stand, and gave me his handkerchief. I wasn't really crying; that would come later in the evening. I was just sniffling a little. He hugged me, and true to his nature as a hustling Hardbub, he invited me to a business lunch with a Raj'Pathani Spice Mogul. I accepted his offer. Marvin, it seemed, was taking the spring semester off for a research project that involved a rather arduous desert.

"Be guided by your light, Aylene. The High Heavens have inscribed on you their sacred blessing."

* * *

Printed in the USA
CPSIA information can be obtained
at www.ICGtesting.com
LVHW061356071023
760211LV00002B/316